The Dark Part of the Sky

A Collection of Bomber Command Ghost Stories

by

Simon Hepworth

WAR STORIES
An imprint of
MENTION THE WAR PUBLICATIONS

First published 2017 by War Stories, an imprint of Mention the War Limited, 32 Croft Street, Farsley, Leeds, LS28 5HA. 'Return Trip' and 'Long Descent' were previously published by Simon Hepworth in 2015 as individual short stories on Kindle.

A CIP catalogue reference for this book is available from the British Library.

ISBN 978-0993336041

Cover design: Topics – The Creative Partnership www.topicsdesign.co.uk
Cover image: Des Knock www.desknock.co.uk

Contents

Introduction.. 8
Return Trip.. 15
Long Descent 49
Duty Carried Out.. 103
Chop Girl 151
Return of the Brylcreem Boys 175

'Which crew position was searching away from the attack, or in the dark part of the sky?'

Combat Report pro-forma issued to bomber crews after a combat, 1944 -45.

To Mandy, my wife and William, my son.

And for Sgt. Pete Gosnold, RAFVR,
killed in action over Germany with four of his crew
on the penultimate operation of their tour,
21st November 1944.

They were just five of the real Brylcreem Boys.

Introduction

I've wanted to write ghost stories about Bomber Command for a while. My previously published books have been squadron histories and a paranormal crime novel, so *The Dark Part of the Sky* is a natural blend of these genres.

Whilst writing *Striking Through Clouds*, the war diary of 514 Squadron RAF, and *Nothing Can Stop Us,* the narrative history of that unit, the scale of crew losses was always at the forefront of my mind; like the rest of Bomber Command a substantial proportion of the squadron's aircrew lost their lives. I am in touch with several veterans and many more members of their families so the loss of these brave men is something I would never consider to be a source of entertainment. As a result, most of these stories are much darker than my novel *Late Shift*, which even gave the Grim Reaper something of a sense of humour.

I ask you to bear in mind that these accounts are not reports of sightings, such as those recounted by the late Bruce Barrymore Halpenny in his comprehensive series of books, *Ghost* Stations. Each of these five tales explores a different aspect of what the bomber boys had to contend with, and there is a germ of truth behind each of them.

Return Trip sees a navigator confront his fear as he and his crew set out for Berlin on another of a seemingly endless series of trips to the Big City. I have endless respect for the courage of the bomber crews and of the night fighter pilots sent up to kill them. I have always wondered how bomber crews gathered the courage to face their task before each flight, knowing the danger they faced. In the words of one such brave pilot, Flying Officer Geoff France, 'You never got used to it, but you coped by not letting other people see how scared you were. It was something you never talked about because if you did, morale would have plummeted. I would have given anything not to have gone out to the aeroplane and climbed into it. Once you got inside you were too busy going through the pre-flight checks to think about anything else.' [1] Five of Geoff France's crew mates, including my great uncle, lost their lives when their Lancaster was shot down over Germany in November 1944. The ultimate accolade for me was to be told by Geoff Payne, retired rear gunner who checked *Return Trip* for technical errors, 'I rode with you all the way.'

Long Descent is inspired by the personal war of my brother-in-law's father, a bomb aimer in a Halifax bomber, was sent to Hamburg on his first two operations. These included the firestorm raid of 28th July 1943. On their first op, they came under attack by a nightfighter. They decided that there must be another way to contribute to the war effort so they volunteered for a move to a Special Duties squadron. This entailed flying alone over the Balkans and Eastern Europe as they dropped agents and supplies to resistance groups. The odds of survival were no better than in the main force. After the war, he was troubled by the thought of the non-combatants caught up in the air raids, and by his direct part in their demise. He was far from alone

---

[1] Quoted in *Hell on Earth* by Mel Rolfe (Grub Street 2001).

in being all too aware that he had caused the deaths of non-combatants, but the overwhelming response from veterans remains 'What alternative was there, with what the Nazis were doing?'

On average, only one crewman in seven escaped from Lancasters when they were shot down. It was not always the bomb aimer, though it might be considered that they were fortunate in lying immediately above the escape hatch; Lancasters were notoriously hard to leave in an emergency. Aircrew faced incredible danger even after surviving the loss of their aircraft and the perils of a parachute descent. They were sometimes shot by troops on the ground as they dangled helpless from their parachute harness. The SS murdered several captured crew men, shooting them out of hand. Mobs of enraged civilians were also prone to lynching downed airmen, particularly if they landed near the target area. It is little wonder that relative safety was to be found only if they were accorded sanctuary by the Luftwaffe. Towards the end of the war, Hitler ordered the execution of captured airmen, just as he had always insisted that Commandos be killed out of hand. Some airmen, particularly those captured by the Gestapo in the company of members of resistance groups or being helped along escape lines, were sent to camps such as Buchenwald to await execution. In one verified case, the allied airmen were only rescued by brave Luftwaffe officers prepared to stand up to the Gestapo and SS.

The infrastructure of death constructed by the Nazi regime is rightly infamous and serves as a warning from history. Auschwitz, Bergen-Belsen, Buchenwald and

Treblinka remain household names in the annals of inhumanity.

The morals of the area bombing strategy have been discussed at inordinate length elsewhere, often in the context of today's ethical standards. I believe it is wholly wrong to judge the aircrew by today's standards of acceptable warfare. They faced the greatest evil of modern times and it must be recognised that there was no other way of taking the war to Germany in the first five years of the war. Had the Nazi machine not been defeated, and this was brought about in no small part by the bombing campaign, countless millions more innocent people would have been murdered by its members. In war, there are rarely easy choices.

Duty Carried Out is written from the perspective of a squadron commander. Bomber Command Squadron COs tended to have two tours of operations behind them, meaning that they were already survivors of countless traumatic experiences before being given a unit to command. Their personal responsibility now included, albeit unwittingly, dealing the fate of hundreds of airmen, dispatching them on missions that are always dangerous and sometimes bordering on suicidal. Their men would, with harrowing inevitability, vanish into the night and rarely was their fate known by their comrades. Even today, more than seven decades later, lost aircraft and their crews are still found and recovered, and at last it is possible to work out what had befallen them.

Each operational incident recounted in *Duty Carried Out* is based on a factual occurrence in the annals of just one unit, 514 Squadron. By extrapolation there must be hundreds of true stories of individual heroism, few of which were recognised officially. The names have been changed and I have given my imagination free rein in recounting exactly what the crews went through but the point is, they did happen.

Chop Girl explores a different facet of squadron life. Wartime romances were commonplace and were not without immense heartbreak. I won't give too much away as I would like you to read the story and form your own view. Suffice it to say, any veteran will confirm that Chop Girls were very real indeed.

The final story, *Return of the Brylcreem Boys*, is intended to be a spot of light relief after the first four accounts. Part of my research included the aforementioned *Ghost Stations* series. As you are embarking on a book of ghost stories, I am sure you either have an interest or belief in the paranormal, or are willing to suspend your disbelief. There are primarily four types of haunting. One of these, demonic hauntings, does not tend to feature at old bomber stations so if you are after that kind of story, try *The Exorcist* instead. Residual hauntings involve no interaction between living and dead, they are simply a recording in which the ghost appears at a specific location with which it had some earthly connection. There are plenty of such sightings at old airfields, with the apparitions seemingly wandering around their old base in accordance with its former layout. Intelligent hauntings feature attempts on the part of the ghost to communicate with the living, often a family member or other person with whom they had a previous connection. These are less common, but are reported, often featuring a phantom airman or woman asking for directions or information. Sometimes they even make telephone calls. Poltergeists tend to cause physical disruption, throwing things around and generally causing mayhem. Whilst they are sometimes attributed to stressed out teenagers and psychokinesis, in the context of the air war, it does not take much of a leap of the imagination to find that they might be the reason behind so many wartime reports of troublesome gremlins.

Brylcreem Boys is a light-hearted attempt on my part to explain the considerable number of sightings and reports of paranormal activity at Bomber Command bases. Consider this for one moment; 55,573 members of Bomber Command were killed in action in World War Two, and another 5,327 died in training accidents. The Runnymede Memorial commemorates over twenty thousand aircrew from the RAF and other Commonwealth air forces who have no known grave. Most of them were from Bomber Command. Predominantly young men, full of life and energy, cut down in immensely traumatic circumstances; where else would their spirits go, and what might they get up to? Once they learnt the various facets of a good haunting, you can easily imagine how tempted they would be to indulge freely. Feel free to prove me wrong…

To the 60,900 who know the truth that we are yet to discover, I offer my utmost respect.

We will remember them.

Simon Hepworth
Leeds, England

Return Trip

1.

'Wake up, you lazy Pommy bastard!'

The words of my room-mate were, as ever, accompanied by the soft thud of a rolled-up pair of flying socks colliding with my head. Garry had, for the past few days, taken to waking me in that rather inconsiderate manner every day. He also insisted on telling me his plans for the evening, even though they never seemed to come to fruition any more.

'If we're not on ops tonight, I'm off to the Bull's Head. Mate, I'm dying for a pint and I'm convinced that the sheila behind the bar fancies me,' he informed me yet again. I had to admire his undying optimism.

'That's a big 'If' and you bloody know it, you daft sod,' I advised him. 'We'll be on ops. We're always on bloody ops and it'll be sodding Berlin again.'

'Yeah, well, I can always live in hope I suppose,' he told me. 'They've got to give us a break some time. I mean, how often do they expect us to visit the damned place? We went there yesterday and the day before, as far as I remember. There can't be much of it left to bomb. We're just moving the bloody rubble from one pile to another.' Garry was sounding more despondent now, and I wished I hadn't spoiled his pipe dream. We didn't have a huge amount to look forward and the occasional raucous night out in the Mess, or a trip to one of Cambridge's hostelries, didn't seem too much to ask. Except that the Royal Air Force felt it had better things for us to do with our time, and we had to do its bidding. We were in this together, along with the other lads in our crew, and the half a hundred other crews in our squadron, all of whom shared our lot.

It had all started so well, I reflected. My interest in flying had started at the age of six or seven when my attention was drawn to a passing aeroplane. The plane, as it growled its way overhead against the backdrop of the grey overcast, was the biggest flying machine I had ever seen. I stopped playing and stared up at it in awe and a degree of wonder. I never knew from whence it came, or its destination, though in all likelihood it took off from one of several military airfields in our area. A twin-engined biplane, I know now, its markings and generally menacing demeanour suggested to me it was a military aircraft. In fact, if my memory serves me correctly, it was a Handley Page Heyford, which is what passed for a heavy bomber in the Royal Air Force in the early Thirties. All I knew at the time was that I wanted to be in it, not underneath it. Be careful what you wish for.

I had to wait quite a while before my first flight. By the time His Majesty graciously allowed me aboard one of his fleet, bombers had become much bigger, infinitely more menacing, and the poor old Heyford had long since been consigned to the scrap heap. I wasn't too perturbed as it meant that I got to play in an Avro Lancaster instead. I even looked forward to ops, but that would soon be knocked out of me.

My childhood was normal, I always thought, but then which child doesn't think that, from their position in the centre of their known universe. My father was an accountant for a printing firm whilst my mother spent every waking hour ministering to the needy, by which I mean her five children. From my father, I inherited a comfortable working relationship with numbers, and a satisfaction in using my head rather than my hands as a way of earning a living. He was a good-humoured man, which cunningly disguised his three years' service on the Western Front. A Captain in the artillery, he had been awarded the Military Cross, though he was reticent about the circumstances. Even before his hearing finally gave up the ghost he had a loud voice, both being a legacy of his time trying to out-shout his battery of howitzers. I had always imagined an accountancy office to be a hushed and academic environment, so perhaps he wandered into the printing press rooms to have a good old bellow at his colleagues. I had not inherited his less-than-dulcet tones, reinforcing my opinion that they were acquired through environment rather than nature.

I was the middle child with an older brother and sister, whilst I was followed with palindromic pedantry by a younger sister then brother. Whilst I don't consider that I caused any of the problems reputedly the remit of middle children, I always harboured a sneaking feeling that my older brother was the heir apparent and the younger was the apple of my father's eye. Much though he undoubtedly loved my sisters, they were girls and therefore did not really count in his grand schemes. Of the three lads, I was probably the most dispensable.

We grew up in the more rural environs of Wiltshire, though my father was still able to commute daily to his number-crunching in Swindon. A cycle ride each morning took him to the nearest station, from where a tank engine would haul my father in a restricted amount of splendour to his work. The good thing for him was that he had all his ledgers in order by late afternoon, so invariably walked into the house at ten to six each evening. Dinner was served at six o'clock precisely. His administrative nature and military service made my father a creature of ingrained habit, and he took us with him through our early lives in this same habitual fashion. The Royal Air Force was to hold no surprises for me in this respect.

As I progressed through my teenage years I retained one desire, which was to become airborne, and developed another, for our neighbour's daughter Alice. Younger than me by six months, Alice and I were classic childhood sweethearts, having been close as friends in primary school and remaining as such even though we went to separate single-sex schools in Swindon. We never really imagined a life apart and, as we matured through our teenage years, we inevitably took more of a physical interest in each other, insofar as that was possible with the constraints of society and our rather traditional families. We had, naturally, talked about getting married and Alice, being extremely sensible, wanted me to get some qualifications and a career. Probably, a riveting life as an accountant beckoned. Even when the war broke out I assumed it would be over before I could take part so flying aeroplanes for a living still did not seem a realistic proposition.

As I approached my eighteenth birthday, the war showed no signs of coming to an end even though the threat of Nazi storm troopers goose-stepping up the high street had now receded. The Battle of Britain had made the RAF by far the most attractive option when it came to laying down your life for your country and I couldn't wait to volunteer. As an adolescent, I couldn't quite aspire to a handlebar moustache and the very thought of me sporting such a facial adornment reduced Alice to a giggling fit whenever I brought the subject up.

Eventually I was old enough to go into Swindon in my best suit and present myself at the recruiting centre. The bluff old sergeant who greeted me read my form, listened to me as I told him my life story, looked at my school exam results and simply said 'Officer material, I expect they'll say. They'll be in touch.' With that he thanked me for volunteering and showed me to the door. As I left the office he said 'I hope you've thought this through properly. All you bright young chaps want to be fighter pilots but what we really need is bomber crews. So as long as you're fit and healthy you've a reasonable chance of being selected, but I wouldn't hold out too much hope of being a pilot. It's more likely they'll train you to be a navigator with your background. You sound like you're happy enough with numbers.'

And so it proved. Within two years I was indeed able to take the lads and our aeroplane half way across the nastier bits of Europe in the dark and get us all back in one piece, all bar any bits and pieces that the enemy defences had managed to shoot off the airframe.

I pulled myself out of my mental navel-gazing. 'I dunno, Garry. It seems we've been going there and back since the dawn of time and for all I know they might keep sending us there till doomsday.' I looked at the alarm clock on the shelf by my bed. Half past one. Great. I'd slept through half the day and the battle order, if there was one, would be posted by now. 'Have you checked the board to see if we're on?' By way of an answer, Garry informed me, somewhat succinctly, that he had not so far seen fit to do so.

2.

We must have got back from Berlin about 0400 hours that morning and after the debrief, breakfast and winding down, I expect I went to bed about seven. These days, though, I could never remember any of the details. The events leading up to take-off and for the first part of the trip were increasingly vague and, more of a worry, I seemed to have developed some form of amnesia as I could never remember anything after we'd bombed and left the target. I hoped to God that I'd been more aware of my surroundings during the trip home, even if my mind was blank now. I'm the navigator, responsible for getting us all out there, delivering a few tons of high explosive and incendiaries, and getting us safely home. We had made it, so it must just be my powers of recollection. Stress, probably. We had that by the bucketful. Anyway, we had been to the Big City so often recently that Dougie, our pilot, probably knew the way by heart. Hell, I expect even our aircraft knew the way. There was an idea. Next time, if it was Berlin again, the Lanc could just do the trip herself and let us go to the boozer.

I sat upright, shifted round and got out of bed and went over to the metal locker that served as a wardrobe. Those of us actively serving His Majesty couldn't just sling our discarded clothing over a chair; everything had its place and for my battle dress uniform that meant hanging in the locker. As an officer, albeit at the lower end of the hierarchy, I was allowed a few privileges, one of which was that an airman usually saw fit to polish my shoes, which I appreciated. They were waiting for me outside the door, gleaming as usual. The lad who did my shoes was yet to be become war weary and cynical and, from my occasional quick chats with him, I knew he looked up to the air crew. He was, he had told me, awaiting re-muster as a flier himself. I felt sorry for him; his cheery demeanour would soon disappear when he realised he had probably signed his own death warrant. Still, there was no point in upsetting him and my shoes were invariably spotless.

I gave myself a quick shave at the sink, a wash and brush up, and my mood slumped yet again as I resigned myself to what I foresaw as the inevitable; another night out over the capital of the Third Reich.

After the recent series of raids, I had started to be troubled by a nightmare. It was always vivid and always the same. I was sitting at my nav table, plotting the latest wind estimates for the return route and deciding whether to risk a cup from my flask of coffee as we left the target area. Suddenly there would be the clatter of six Browning machine guns as both turrets opened fire, a desperate shout from one of the gunners: 'FIGHTER!! CORKSCREW PORT, GO!!' followed by a blood-curdling scream which ended, chillingly, as suddenly as it started. It was accompanied by the racket of exploding cannon shells around me, my flask shattering as it was struck by passing ammunition, and a feeling of falling in the dark. Then, invariably, I would wake up. I suppose I ought to be grateful to Garry for the comedy sock routine which always interrupted my headlong plummet towards oblivion. Coupled with my repeated bouts of homeward-bound amnesia, it was probably no surprise that I was beginning to worry if my sanity would last until the end of my tour.

I faced a bit of a dilemma; if I went to see the quack he might tell me to get a grip, maybe muttering darkly about the unendurable stigma of 'LMF', Lack of Moral Fibre, the official term for cowardice. Although he didn't fly himself, he held the rank of Squadron Leader and was therefore on equal, and indeed friendly, terms with my flight commander. A word in my direct superior's ear would mark me down as a shirker or, worse, a coward. That kind of black mark could easily blight the rest of my career, should I live long enough to have one. On the other hand, he knew us all well, those who had survived more than a few ops, so he might be sympathetic and diagnose sinusitis which would ground me for a few days as I wouldn't be fit to fly. It happened occasionally, and there was a chance that he would give me that respite rather than see me go round the bend. The downside would be that my crew would carry on with their tour, albeit with another navigator, and they'd finish before me. If, that is, my replacement knew which way the pilot should point the Lancaster so it got to the target. And then, on my return, I would probably be inserted into a sprog crew and the odds of me living to tell the tale would plummet faster than the plane in my bad dream.

Along with the dreams came an increasing sense of foreboding, a growing sense of conviction that I wasn't going to make it. So far, we had had a quiet tour, with little to rattle us, though we had seen other aircraft explode or go down in flames along the route and the demented inferno of flak all around us over target. But we had, whisper it quietly, so far been lucky and had outlived many of our contemporaries. None of us counted the losses even though we thought we knew the bigger picture and the BBC was quite happy to tell the waiting world how many of our number failed to return from each raid. The senior ranks at Group, Bomber Command HQ and the Air Ministry didn't seem too keen to discuss how to reduce the butcher's bill with us and they got a bit sniffy with anyone who thought to bring up the subject at briefing. I couldn't think why; it was not as if I was likely to think of asking the station telephonist to patch me through to Reichsmarschall Hermann Goering so I could share the joy with him. I figured that our losses each time out seemed to average about one aircraft missing from every twenty or so despatched and each empty chair in the Mess, and empty dispersal pan, told its own story.

We didn't talk about it, of course. It was considered a frightfully bad show to mention The Chop. Faces came and went, but we never knew the other lads. They might easily not have existed. We would have a good few beers in the Officer's Mess, or clear off as a crew to the more relaxed atmosphere of the Bull's Head where we could let our hair down a bit more.

Our crewmembers hailed from a variety of backgrounds. Dougie, from York, along with Garry, who was the Bomb

Aimer and I were Flying Officers, almost the lowest rung amongst the commissioned officer fraternity. The other chaps were Sergeants. Alan, the Flight Engineer, was a soft-spoken lad from Merthyr Tydfil whilst the Wireless Operator, Joe, was a strident South African. His real name, he once confided, was Johannes which he felt was a tad German for comfort. Half-Afrikaner, he was one hundred percent behind the war effort, as evidenced by his sticking his neck on the line every time we headed out over the North Sea. Our backs were watched by the two gunners, known to the rest of us on the quiet as Tweedle Dum and Tweedle Dee. Those were not their real names but both were short, dark-haired and slight in stature and might conceivably have been brothers. They were really called Bill and Pete, and they shared an intense mutual interest in gardening. Pete had been trying to persuade the Station Commander to allow an allotment to be set up behind one of the hangars where there was a piece of rough land that might do more, he argued, to contribute to the war effort. The Station Commander had yet to reach a decision.

We had been together since the Operational Training Unit, apart from Alan Johnson joined us a few weeks later. We'd been training on Wellington aircraft, retired bombers, and they didn't need a Flight Engineer. Once we got onto heavies, the spanner monkeys were suddenly needed and Alan joined our merry throng, having decided he would rather fly ops than stay down the mines. I thought his choice was academic as both jobs involved not inconsiderable danger and precious little daylight.

Since our posting to RAF Elmsford in the East Anglian fen country, my log book showed twenty-four ops. We should have done twenty-six but had to turn back twice, due to engine problems and a knackered intercom. Both were no-go items, though this didn't stop some of the 'press-on-regardless' chaps. There weren't many of those, but that might just be because, for them, the attitude had proved suicidal. I remembered then that my own logbook was in the Navigation Leader's office as he checked and signed it each month. It would by now be a few trips behind. Updating it would wait. Again, the bureaucratic tail wagged the dog. He was probably checking to see if I'd been taking shortcuts on the route to Berlin; not that there was much chance of that. For the past few trips the big wigs had stuck to the same cunning plan which saw us taking a direct route to Berlin with no discernible deviation. That would outwit Jerry, I thought. He'll never believe we would keep that up so would most likely send his night fighters to Munich just in case in we were really planning to go there instead. Funny how he hadn't yet thought of that, though. Every bloody night they were waiting for us in the same place. It saved petrol for both sides, which was something.

All in all, I decided I would be better off keeping my mouth shut about my personal concerns and just getting on with the job. Twenty-four completed ops from our tour of thirty meant we were eighty percent of the way to a period of calm, at least for six months. Screening off ops did not actually mean we were safe; there was still a war on and a posting to training school to look after the new boys would place us in the hands of the chronically inexperienced. In our world, if you learned from experience your odds of survival improved dramatically, from non-existent to merely woeful. By my reckoning we could, at the start of our tour, expect to survive twenty ops and we had done that and more. We only had to survive another six to have a chance of a long break, and who knows when the war might end? It was January 1944 and there was an expectation that Allied boots would be on European soil before too long. It might all be over by Christmas.

3.

It wasn't too late for lunch, as long as we didn't hang about, but our plans for the rest of the day, possibly the remainder of our lives, hinged on the answers to a two-part question. One: was there an ops battle order posted? And two: was our crew on it? Based on the past few days' experience it would be a quiet but firm 'Yes' to both of those, but I felt we were due for a bit of good luck. We didn't often fly more than three nights running. The weather usually saw to that, and even the chair-borne warriors at Group felt that it was useful for us to have a breather every so often. Battle fatigue was expensive on aircraft, and it was nice to think that they would occasionally spare a thought for the crews.

Garry and I sauntered over to the 'A' Flight office. There were a few people coming and going; some of the other crews greeted us in passing but most just ignored us, almost looking straight through us. A constant stream of fresh faces turned up to replace those who were lost and, to them, we were probably just a couple of old lags who probably wouldn't be around much longer.

The board was adorned with a fresh piece of paper listing those of us lucky enough to be blessed with the chance of getting ourselves wiped out this very evening. Sure enough, there we were, listed under our aircraft designator, a simple 'L'. L-Love was her call sign. She had a serial number, as did we all, and that would stay with her for as long as she stayed 'on charge' in the Royal Air Force. Her squadron code might change occasionally but, since we'd been assigned to her, she had always been A6-L. The chaps thought L-Love was a bit soft, so Dougie had christened her L-Lass and arranged for the name 'Top Lass' to be painted on her nose, along with a suitable portrait of a well-endowed female gleefully throwing bombs at a cowering Nazi with a toothbrush moustache. I wondered how many beers that had cost him to bribe an artistic fitter. Dougie told us that the female was an accurate caricature of his wife back in Yorkshire. Garry had told him to dream on.

Briefing was at 1600 hours for navigators, so that we could plot the route on a nice large, flat, table before taking off. It made life so much easier. Main briefing was at 1700 hours so, I presumed, we would take-off around 2000 hours. That had been the pattern recently and it would give us an hour or so to grab something to eat before festivities commenced. That was unless Dougie fancied a trip round the block by way of a Night Flying Test.

We went to give our pilot a shout, not wanting him to miss the fun. He was, as usual, lying in his bed gradually adjusting to being awake. 'We're on, mate,' Garry told him. 'Briefing's in a couple of hours. Are we taking the old bird out for a trip round the countryside or shall we just go and get some nosh? The choice is yours, cobber.'

'She was fine when we parked her so she'll be alright, as long as the ground crew haven't lent her to some other lot in the mean time to take her out for a spin. Give me ten minutes to get ready. I'll check with the flight office about Lass and then I'll be with you. I'll see you in the Mess.'

It wasn't far from the Officers' Accommodation block to the Mess itself; in that respect, we had it easier than the Sergeants, who had to hike half a mile from their Nissen huts to the NCOs' own mess. The riff-raff weren't deemed suitable to eat with the officers, even though each night we depended on each other for our lives. We couldn't socialise on the station either so the seven of us routinely cleared off to neutral territory whenever we could. We were close-knit, and sod the class distinction inherent to the RAF.

By the time our aeroplane driver had stirred from his pit and joined us in the entrance to the Dining Hall, there were a few other bods hanging around waiting for a table. We had WAAF waitresses to cater for our every reasonable need; unfortunately, it was left to them to decide what was reasonable. Garry's earthier needs had long-since been categorised as not strictly desirable, let alone reasonable, by many of the young ladies he had made them to.

As before, we chatted with some of the more familiar crews, including several I couldn't remember having seen for quite a while. In fact, I could have sworn blind more than a few had been reported missing. It was a tremendous relief to see them back in the Mess, acting like they'd never been away. They had, I presumed, evaded capture, or had simply landed their damaged aircraft elsewhere, whilst perhaps some had been away on leave. I asked one of my fellow navigators, whom I thought had failed to return a couple of weeks earlier, but he told me he hadn't been away and put it down to us just not being on the same ops. I wondered if it was yet another symptom of my crumbling mental faculties. However, it gave me some hope; if these lads I had thought lost had eventually turned up safe and sound, maybe the true chop figures weren't as bad as I'd reckoned. I mentioned this to Garry, who just looked out of the window at the leaden sky and said vaguely 'When your number's up, mate, that's it,' before changing the subject to a reasoned discourse on the menu.

My feeling of gloom and despondency had been suppressed by the company of my mates, especially the irrepressible Garry, but I must confess it was still there, gnawing away at me. I had always felt the tension before ops, we all did, but today my mouth was even drier than normal, my stomach unsettled, neither of which boded well for the forthcoming trip. Stomach problems would be a complete and utter disaster; if I was caught short then, encumbered as I was by layers of thick flying clothing, I would be lucky to make it to the aircraft's Elsan, which was our only toilet onboard, in time to meet my body's sudden need. It would also mean I was away from my post for the duration of my personal emergency, which Dougie would go on about endlessly until one of the other lads annoyed him, and I would also have to play catch up with finding our position when I was fit to continue. I toyed briefly, once again, with going to the Sick Bay but just couldn't bring myself to do it. Maybe Garry was right, I considered; if it's your turn there's nothing you can do about it. Then I comforted myself with the thought, as ever, that we would be OK. It was always another crew that bought it. Twenty-four down, six to go.

Bacon and egg was a rare luxury for most people but for us fearless fliers it was a regular repast, just so long as we were on ops. We always had it before a sortie, it was something of a ritual. Just recently, though, the meal had become tasteless. It was a treat for us, the RAF seemed to think. Those who are about to die, we salute you.

For me, though, the meal was tarnished by association. Imagine being locked in a room, where a tray of thirty eggs sits on a table. It's a massive room. It takes you two or three hours to walk across it, in pitch black. You are told that if you want to be let out, you must eat all thirty eggs, one at a time. After each egg, the lights go out and you must walk through it to the far side, where there is a roaring fire. There are a few hundred of you wandering across the room, unable to see each other unless you are very close. You might bump into someone else at any time unless you are extremely careful. To make matters worse, in one hand you have a bottle of petrol and in the other a hand grenade, from which the pin has been removed. When you get to the fire at the far side, you simply throw your grenade into it, mindful that you might get hit by someone else's at any moment, and then you walk for two or three hours back across the room.

As if that wasn't stressful enough, there will be people shooting at you, especially near the roaring fire where, in any case, you are much easier to see. And away from the fire, you know that there are a couple of hundred bogeymen somewhere in the room with you, there, lurking in the dark, waiting with a nasty weapon to bludgeon you. It's like a kid's worst nightmare. But each bogeyman is very real, and he's got a radar operator, and he can see you in the dark, and the pilot can see the flames of your exhaust, and if that's not enough they've got fighter flares, or else the searchlights illuminate the clouds beneath you, or the fires you have worked so hard to ignite show up your aircraft so you are exposed to their searching gaze. If you use a device to try and see him before he sees you, he can detect that and follow its beam and it will lead him right to you. And when the bogeyman sees you, he hasn't got a cudgel, but instead he's got some 20mm cannon and he is going to blow you to hell. You know what's coming, but you just don't know when. So that's why now I don't like eggs and it's why I'm shit-scared of the dark.

It might appear that, by this time, I was on the point of breaking down, collapsing on the table with my head in my hands, blubbering like a terrified child. It wasn't quite like that. This was fear, not abject, screaming terror. Outwardly I remained calm. We all did, it was what was expected of us. We would have been stark raving mad not to feel scared, though. Terror, leading to panic, was entirely different. The fear I felt was kept inside, locked in by the unspoken support of my pals who were all, I had no doubt, sharing the same emotion, and by the rigid hierarchy within which we existed. I could still function as a normal human being, even if normality for me entailed navigating a heavy bomber across half of Europe and bombing its cities.

'Are you going to eat your breakfast, or just sit there staring at it? Some poor bloody chook has given up her offspring to feed you, not to mention the porker whose number came up to supply the bacon.' Garry had obviously retained his appetite despite the growing tension ahead of briefing.

It would have sent out the wrong signals if I had handed over my breakfast to my crew mate, so I overcame my reluctance and finished the plateful. A cup of tea also helped, but then again, I had never known a brew to fail in this respect.

4.

I hated having to kill time before the briefings. There were a thousand things I would prefer to do on what might be my last day on Earth; top of the list was a range of activities with a host of obliging young ladies, but these are best left to the imagination. After that, a concert, hiking in some of England's magnificent scenery, and an evening in the pub would do the job. Unfortunately, as the station was sealed before ops, none of these were on offer. No one got in or out without a chit and telephone calls were prohibited. There was no point, when all's said and done, in giving Jerry advanced warning that we were going to do exactly the same thing that we had done for the last few nights. He would find out soon enough. I joined Dougie and Garry in cycling out to dispersal to make sure our aeroplane was fit for the job ahead.

Top Lass was sitting where we had left her earlier this morning, no doubt brooding over the coming night. If machines have feelings I expect hers were no different from ours; she rarely showed it apart from the occasional technical hiccup when she really didn't want to play. Lass was ahead of us in experience, having survived thirty-seven trips over enemy territory. Each was celebrated by a bomb painted above her name and caricature. Our squadron, unlike some, tended to allocate crews a specific aircraft. They probably thought it inspired a sense of ownership and hence we would be more likely to bring the plane back. Every so often a crew whose own steed was playing up or damaged would borrow a Lanc if her own crew wasn't on the battle order. All too frequently neither aircraft nor crew were ever heard from again, so we preferred to stick with our own.

Dougie chatted to the ground crew chief, a Flight Sergeant who answered, perhaps inevitably, to 'Chiefy'. He had turned up recently, probably having been posted to the squadron, though he never talked about why. These things happened in the RAF. Despite his brief period with us, Chiefy already believed that Lass was his own private property and was not afraid to chide Dougie and the rest of us if we brought her back with holes in. For the most part we had, thus far, looked after her. In the absence of the rest of the crew, Dougie was resolute in his decision not to air-test Lass before the op. 'She was sweet as a bird again last night, Chiefy. Not a flicker on the instruments.'

'That's Rolls-Royce for you, sir. Nothing but the best for King and Country.' Chiefy's tone suggested a hint of irony; God only knew how many cold, wet hours he and his team worked to keep Lass airworthy. 'She's knocking on a bit, this old girl. You sure you don't want to trade her in for a younger model?'

'I don't think the RAF would let us do that. There's no second-hand market for a used Lanc. One careless owner isn't much of a selling point. No, thanks Chiefy, we'll stick with her for as long as she'll let us.' Dougie and the Flight Sergeant wandered off to stare at Top Lass's nether regions and give her a poke or a prod as they saw fit. I wasn't one of those navigators who had failed pilot training, so it was all a black art to me. I was happy to work out where we were now, how to get to where we needed to be and how long it would take us. It was far less grief.

The navigators' briefing was a civilised, almost perfunctory, affair. There was absolutely no surprise when the target was revealed as Berlin once more. As I had cynically predicted, the route was identical. I mentioned this to the bod next to me, whom I recognised having sat next to him the previous night. 'It's always the same now,' he confirmed. 'They seem to think it's easier to manage, or something. I'm sure Butch knows what he's doing.' I told him we might as well just use the same charts day in, day out and save ourselves the bother of plotting the same route each time. He laughed and offered me a smoke, which I accepted gratefully. We all smoked before ops; it was another way of coping with the stress.

I wished I shared my colleague's confidence in the C-in-C of Bomber Command, but it was good to know it wasn't just me who had picked up on this seemingly bizarre, if not potentially lethal, tactic. At the end of the day, though, it was not my place to question these things. HQ at High Wycombe decided these things and my role was to do what I was told, when I was told to do it. Butch, or Air Chief Marshal Sir Arthur Harris as he was more properly titled, certainly knew his own mind, but whether this was synonymous with knowing what he was doing was always open for quiet debate. We knew where we stood with the man, even if we never actually got to see him. He seemed to support us, even as he sent us out every night to carry death and destruction to the enemy, whilst facing our own demise along with it.

Once we had done our route planning we moved through to the main briefing room. As usual we were sworn to secrecy as the senior officers loved the element of surprise as they drew back the curtain to announce that yes, it was Berlin again. I found Dougie, Garry and the lads who were sitting at our usual spot at the back of the room. I couldn't shake off the sense of *déjà vu* as it continued to move remorselessly to the forefront of my mind. The feeling of foreboding grew with it, something that I had never truly experienced before. I had heard of other bods experiencing a premonition of their own impending loss, but I had never truly believed in its stark reality. What happened, I wondered, to all those who had such a conviction but who survived? How did they talk their way out of their insistence that they wouldn't come back, when they'd been proved wrong? Once again, premonitions were rarely spoken of amongst our number.

It being his show the squadron CO, who was a Wing Commander with two tours behind him, drew back the briefing curtain to an unappreciative groan from our number. 'I'm impressed mate, how did you guess that?' muttered Garry to me with undisguised irony. The CO was respected by us as a good leader, who was prepared to stick his neck out as far as he expected us to. Tonight, he told us, he would be flying with a sprog crew, rather than send them out as inexperienced lambs to almost inevitable slaughter. He didn't phrase it quite like that, however. I remembered he'd done the same on the past few ops, and in doing so must have known the huge risk he was taking. We had our twenty-four ops under our belts; the Wingco had more than twice that number.

The briefing ground on remorselessly, our section leaders updating us on the various specialisms of our collective trade. Turning points, target indicators, signals, weather, flak dispositions; each piece of information had the potential to affect our futures. And then it was time to earn our flight pay.

Much of what followed the briefing was routine, borne out of necessity. The RAF had its processes, its rituals and its rules. If there's a routine you don't need to worry about what to do next and the whole thing becomes second nature. After a while you get to depend on the routine and eventually it morphs into superstition, especially if you're facing death every time you go through the process. It's human nature to want the same kit, collect it in the order, get into the same lorry and have the same driver to take you to dispersal. It worked last time and the time before so if you're going to come back safely this time, everything needs to be just the same as previously. Irrational obsession was a secondary consideration compared with stacking the odds in your favour. On this occasion, everything was as it should be, no one stirred up my personal demons by upsetting the order of things, and for this I was truly grateful.

Our crew traditions continued when we reached the dispersal pan and waddled over to Top Lass, weighed down with kit. This we stowed; flasks, rations, parachutes, and the equipment specific to our role. In my case it was a nav bag, chart and pencils. Then we clambered back out as we still had time to kill. A few last cigarettes, the orange tips glowing bright against the darkness of this far-flung outpost of the airfield; they would be as nothing compared to the inferno of light we knew we might well see before long. Searchlights, tracer, exploding flak and perhaps, if the cloud was sufficiently thin, the fire bed of a burning city. If our mates were unlucky there would be the bright multi-hued conflagration of a bomber exploding as petrol, rubber, aluminium, amatol and human bodies combined in a brief but diabolical firework display. Awesome, it was, and terrible too, and repeated far too many times but, to our private shame, each fireball was shared by a sense of relief that it was somebody other than us. They couldn't get us all, so every time it was their bomber rather than ours, the chances of us making it home seemed to rise.

It was nearly time to board, so we gathered round Lass's tail wheel, unbuttoned our flying suits and gave it a soaking for good luck. The old girl never seemed to mind. Then we took our places. I was luckier than most, especially those of a sensitive disposition, as I had a curtain to shut me off from the hellish reality outside. Unless I needed to shoot the stars through the astrodome, I could pretend I was somewhere else. The other chaps were paid to look out of the window, though Joe was technically employed to listen. He did double up as spare gunner though so had to do his share of staring out at the proceedings.

'Form up over Southwold,' I told Dougie over the intercom when we were settled. 'For a change.' That much was to be expected. We had almost always used that coastal town as a mustering point as we set out over the North Sea. To get there at our assigned altitude of 21,000 feet we would head for Birmingham and then double back. A Lancaster with five tons of bombs and sufficient fuel for a return trip to Berlin would not exactly climb like a homesick angel. I'd got Gee equipment to plot our position, at least as far as the German border, and possibly further if the enemy didn't manage to jam it. After that we were dependent on my skill as a navigator to guide Dougie to the target and back.

The peace and tranquility of my work space was suddenly disturbed by the roar as the first of Lass's four Merlin engines started up. I didn't usually pay too much attention to that procedure as Dougie and Alan had it all down to a fine art and it wasn't something that involved the rest of us. I just had to make sure my own instruments and equipment was present, correct and functioning. The racket increased in proportion to the number of Lass's engines that were up and running. When all four were thundering away it was hard to hear yourself think and there was a tendency to try and shout over the intercom, even though our voices were amplified. As with everything else, though, we adjusted to the environment and filtered it out. On a couple of occasions, we had to shut down an engine in-flight and the reduction in volume was unnerving. All in all, I preferred to put up with the din of all four Merlins.

'Pilot to Navigator.' We were formal now, and would remain so for most of the trip, unless something unusual happened. Intercom discipline bred crew discipline, and a disciplined crew was professional and might, just might, live longer. Therefore, we cut the banter when we were flying.

'Navigator to pilot, go ahead.'

'Pilot to Navigator, all set?'

'Navigator to pilot, all set.' Dougie then repeated his call to our colleagues, ensuring that the intercom was working and that no one raised any last-minute objections to the idea of stirring up the hornets' nest that was the Luftwaffe's night fighter defences. The noise from the engines increased as Lass edged forward then I felt a familiar lurch as Dougie applied the brakes. We stopped for quite a while, seemingly held up by some unseen problem, unseen by me, that was, sitting down in the cheap seats next to Joe. After a couple of minutes, I stuck my head around the bulkhead and looked up to the flight deck. Dougie and Alan were seemingly waiting for a gap in the line of Lancasters rolling past us.

'Problems, gentlemen?' I enquired.

'No bugger's letting us in,' Garry drawled laconically, doubtless from his unofficial take-off position in the nose. 'That's fine by me. You carry on chaps.'

'Someone always used to back off a bit, as we're none of us in any rush. But the last few times it looks like they can't wait,' Dougie informed the rest of us. Eventually, Lass roared again and we moved forward.

'We're right at the back of the taxi rank now,' added Bill from his seat in the rear turret. Along with Pete, who sat tonight in the mid-upper position, he would spend virtually the whole trip facing backwards. I wondered if they got disorientated when they got on a bus, unless it was reversing at speed, in which case they would feel quite at home.

'Pilot to crew, going on green,' said Dougie as we paused again, evidently waiting for the green lamp to shine from the control caravan at the end of the runway.

For a while nothing happened, then Alan broke in. 'The dozy bastards are going home! Can't they see us sitting here?'

Dougie must have looked past Alan as he joined in. 'What the hell are they doing? Is the caravan on fire or something?'

'No. They've just packed up and got out of the van for a leg stretch.' Looking up at the flight deck I saw him slide back the panel in the window and heard him shout something. If they couldn't see the Lanc and hear the Merlins, I thought they were hardly likely to respond to a bloke shouting out of a window that was twenty feet off the ground. And so it proved, as they took no notice whatsoever.

Dougie had clearly lost patience, and probably his sense of humour. 'Pilot to Rear Gunner. Clear above and behind?'

'Rear Gunner here, clear above and behind, skipper,' Bill replied. Once more the engines roared and Lass edged forward, then began to accelerate as her props bit the chilly night air. I wasn't entirely sure that this was proper procedure, but then again, the airfield control staff clearing off with a fully-laden Lancaster parked next to them probably didn't feature in the Airfield Procedures Manual, or whatever rules they ran by, either. I figured Dougie probably knew what he was doing; he was quite likely as hyped up as the rest of us and had probably decided to argue the toss when, or more likely if, we got back. We had more to worry about for the next eight hours than a breach of procedure, and assuming we didn't crash or collide with another aircraft whilst still in the vicinity of the runway, Dougie would probably tell them he saw a green. Alan would back him up; we all would. It was, for now, us against the world.

5.

We went to war, seven men amongst a few thousand, opposed by several million Germans, many of whom were in possession of seriously offensive weapons. We droned through the cloud layers, occasional turbulence causing Lass to buck and sway, sometimes to lurch and drop, but the altimeter by my desk slowly wound its way upwards. I focused on taking Gee readings and plotting these on my map, then comparing forecast winds with actuals. For once, the Met. people had been reasonably accurate and I had no cause for complaint. We crossed the North Sea and, when my Gee plots showed that we were a couple of minutes from crossing the Dutch coast, I advised my colleagues, 'Enemy coast ahead,' as countless navigators had done before and, I have no doubt, since.

With dense cloud beneath us, several thousand feet thick, there was no way the searchlights could have any effect whatsoever. They didn't even light the clouds to provide a backdrop for us to crawl across. So far, so good.

It couldn't last, and it didn't. Halfway across Holland, the duck shoot started. The Wing Commander was the first to go, by our reckoning. He'd signalled to us by lamp as we crossed the English coastline and we had then flown in parallel, separated by a few hundred feet laterally. That was safe enough; we each knew where the other was. In the starlight, we could occasionally make out other bombers but, to my mind, there were far fewer of them than I'd expected. Normally there would have been ten or fifteen bombers for every one we saw tonight. Maybe this was a diversionary raid, and our squadron, along with possibly one or two others, had been sent to Berlin whilst the Main Force went off somewhere else. If that was the case, I hoped the night fighters didn't fall for the ruse. Better that someone else should bear the brunt.

'Hell's teeth…' That was from Garry. 'The Wingco's just blown up.'

Looking up to the front I could see the fading glow of the explosion reflected on the inside of the cockpit perspex. That was it; no more shepherding and nursemaiding sprog crews from our fearless leader. He'd been a good type, and that would probably have to serve as his epitaph. As for the lads with him we neither knew nor could we get too worked up. We'd lost too many friends to grieve for those we didn't even know.

A flamer a short while later, a bomber burning as it fell, showed us that the bogeymen were still with us and in numbers, then another explosion took a third crew to meet their Maker. When the fourth fell, as we crossed into German territory, my bad feeling returned with a vengeance. Ten percent of the force destroyed, by my count, and we were not even half way to the target. The diversion must be working as the night fighters were definitely amongst us.

The carnage continued as explosions and flames periodically reminded us of our own mortality. It was usual practice for the navigator to log these, to help with accounting for missing crews on our return. I kept adding to my list, which was twenty entries long by the time we reached Berlin. The target focused our minds on our task, despite the local flak barrage adding to the nastiness surrounding us.

'Steady, steady.... bombs gone.' Lass leapt for the heavens as Garry pressed the bomb release button and unleashed our contribution to the redevelopment of Berlin. An agonising wait for the photoflash, to prove we had really had gone to the Big City, as opposed to carpet-bombing Grimsby, and we turned for home.

I went through my wind calculations and thought about a cup of coffee. Maybe, just maybe, I'd overreacted, I thought, mentally cursing myself for going soft. Then my nightmare moved from dream to reality. Bill and Pete opening fire on something simultaneously, the truncated scream in the intercom, my flask shattering and it all going dark. My parachute was stowed next to my table but it might have been on the moon for all the use it was. Lass was plummeting earthwards, spinning now. Far from the darkness I had imagined in my dream there was an orange glow in the flight deck, probably from one or more engines blazing merrily away.

I knew that this was no dream. I couldn't move, my body weight massively increased by the g-forces caused by

Lass's death roll. The old girl wouldn't make the end of the war and neither would we. Somehow, I felt calm. There was, after all, nothing I could do to escape so no point at all in panicking.

I closed my eyes, thought of Alice and all our unrealised plans, and waited for the end.

6.

'Wake up, you lazy Pommy bastard!'

The thud of Garry's socks against my forehead disturbed my personal peace, as was his intention. 'If we're not on tonight, I'm off to the Bull's Head. Mate, I'm dying for a pint and I'm convinced that the sheila behind the bar fancies me.'

Here we go again, I thought. Something was not quite right; I could by now predict what Garry was going to say. This time, in addition, my dream seemed too vivid, far too real. And my day was starting in precisely the same way as the last few had done. I was getting a bit bemused, to put it mildly.

'Garry,' I asked. 'Do you ever get a feeling that we've been here before?'

'Course we've been here before, you drongo. We were here yesterday, because we bloody live here.' But this time there seemed in his voice to be an evasiveness that I hadn't noticed previously, and he came across as unusually defensive.

'That's not what I mean. This is starting to drive me round the bend. You wake me up by throwing those mangy old socks at me, then go on about that girl at the Bull's

Head. Don't you feel it too, mate?' I wanted Garry to tell me I was wrong, but this time his silence was no reassurance. 'We're just doing the same thing day in, day out, aren't we?'

Garry paused, standing at the window, contemplating God alone knew what. He turned to look at me. 'Yeah well there's no point in denying that, I suppose. I still hoped I was wrong, mate. I sincerely thought I was going mad and I certainly wanted that to be the case, but I reckon you've cottoned on too. We *are* on ops every night, and it's *always* to Berlin. The same times and route too. We would never normally do that; in fact, it's bloody suicide, it's obvious to anyone with an ounce of common sense, even those chairborne warriors at HQ.

'The food is always the same and it's tasteless. We're not really eating it, it's just that we remember eating it. And I know you've noticed that the new bods who ignore us. They are nothing to do with us now, they can't see us and they don't know we are here. Same with those Lancs that wouldn't let us in, and the control people pissing off while we are waiting to go. It's like we're invisible, because we are bloody invisible. It's only our old mates that bother with us and, you know what? At one time or another they've all been posted missing.

'It took a while for the penny to drop with me. I started getting this dream night after bloody night. I release the bombs over the target indicators. Bloody bang on they were too, probably the best yet. We wait for the photo flash to go off, and that's interminable. Dougie turns away and we leave the target. Then it's bedlam as one of the lads shouts for Dougie to corkscrew but he's too bloody late.

Pete, I think it is, screams and there's cannon shells all over the place. I don't know what happens to you but I've got my chute on so I don't hang around. I open the hatch and go through it. But my chute won't open as it's been shredded by the Jerry fighter's bullets so I just get a panoramic view of Berlin coming towards me at terminal velocity. Bloody exciting in any other circumstances but not when you've got a load of parachute silk trailing out behind you that's as much use as a bloody chocolate teapot. Then I wake up same as the previous day, and it all starts again. Do you get it now, mate? We're ghosts. We got the chop the other night, or last week, or it might be last year for all I know. The only people who see us and talk to us are the other bods who bought it, either before or since. They didn't miraculously come back to us; we've joined them, not the other way around. I reckon even Chiefy has passed over as well, he was certainly never around before all this nonsense started.

'Each night the Wingco announces he's coming to Berlin with us and he's always the first to get the chop. Then they all fall in the same order. I see a lot more from the nose than you can from back there. There's only about forty planes with us and it's the same forty, night after night. Then we get hit by the same fighter, at the same time in the same place; Pete gets it first then we are going down, spinning. None of us survives, which is why we're all here. And then it all starts again, day after bloody day. For all I know, we are going to spend eternity doing the same trip time and again, always hoping to finish it but never getting home, then we wake up and have to do it all over again. Long after the war is over, and all we see around us has been abandoned, we will still set off for Berlin each night, us and the other forty-odd aircraft that bought it the same night. It's like The Flying Dutchman with a Lancaster. Every night we will fail to return. We'd better get used to it. Now, like I keep saying, I'm dying for a pint…'

Long Descent

'Left...left...steady.' Flying Officer Robbie Ticknall gave his instructions in measured tones, his concentration on his task managing to shut out the bedlam outside. Straight and level over the hotly-defended target, the Lancaster bomber would be easy meat for any flak gunner who got it in his sights. The few minutes whilst the aircraft ran in to the aiming point were usually the tensest of the trip, except for those occasions when the aircraft was under fire.

'One these days you're going to say back a bit and the Skipper will have to put the darned aeroplane in reverse.' The flat Canadian tone could only have come from the rear turret where Sgt Hank Murray hid his nerves with banter. Even so it was almost unheard of for anyone to interrupt the proceedings at this stage of the trip.

'Cut the chatter and let the Bomb Aimer do his job.' Flight Lieutenant Ron Hebdon's terse voice seemed to have risen an octave in the stress of the moment.

'Steady...right one degree...steady...bombs gone!' The target indicators, replenished by the backers-up, were visible through his bomb sight as Robbie pressed the bomb release button and the Lancaster lurched upwards, as if shrugging off her load. The pilot trimmed his aircraft to allow for the entirely new weight and load distribution, and kept her plodding along the same line. Thirty seconds of steady flight whilst they awaited the white light of the photo flash was all that the crew now had to endure before breaking away from the target. Thirty interminable seconds whilst the red and orange glow of the inferno they had raised did its level best to expose them to the gaze of those who dearly wished to kill them.

They were, technically, over Frankfurt, but the hellish panorama beneath, to the sides and behind them bore no resemblance to the city that had evolved over time to become a powerhouse of industry. The factories were impossible to distinguish from the surrounding houses, the civic buildings and the medieval quarter. Robbie knew that his bombs could be hitting anything but at that exact moment he didn't care. They were now above the centre of the burning city and he knew that as soon as they had taken the obligatory bombing photo the Skipper would put the Lancaster into a dive to increase their airspeed and they would run for the darkness that waited tantalisingly to embrace them.

There was the flak. Bright flashes then a dark smudge against the fiery backdrop. The explosions as the shells burst was mostly lost in the din of the engines, which pervaded even the protection of the crew's leather helmets. Only the closer bursts were audible and even then, the airmen were spared the sinister rattle of shrapnel against the metal skin of the fuselage, the tapping of the Grim Reaper's fingernails against the fraction of an inch of aluminium that was their only protection.

Searchlights, bright beams seemingly reaching to the heavens, probed and swept across the sky, seeking the careless, unwary or simply unfortunate. When a light found a victim, its fellows swarmed to join in, the aeroplane, a bright point like an artificial star, moving erratically as the pilot tried every manoeuvre he knew, and some made up in the desperation of the moment. The flak followed the searchlights and, almost inevitably, there would be a diabolical firework display as the bomber erupted and fell to earth.

The aircraft bucked and swayed as she made her tortuous way through the turbulent air, vertical currents from the fires clutching at her as she fought for the sanctuary beyond. 'Twenty seconds gone, skipper,' Robbie called out. A few more seconds and the camera would prove to the satisfaction of the desk wallahs that the crew had bombed the target as they were paid to do. The comforting darkness beyond the conflagration that was Frankfurt seemed closer now, almost within their grasp, even though they should be directly over the centre of the target when the flash went off. As an experienced crew, they knew that they would not be allowed to get away with bombing on the edge of the flames and that the 'fringe merchants' who bombed and broke away early were no more likely to emerge unscathed than those whose bottle allowed them to drop their explosive load accurately. The safety of the surrounding darkness was, Robbie knew, illusory. Beyond the flak and the searchlights lurked the night fighters, dreadful sharks of the air, equipped with the latest technology that German ingenuity could devise. They never gave any warning of their approach; at you could always see the flak and searchlights, which rarely crept up silently on you.

'There's the flash. Take us home, Skipper.'

'Navigator to pilot. Steer two eight zero.' Robbie breathed a sigh of relief as the Lancaster banked to the left. Through his Plexiglas bubble in the nose of the aeroplane he could still make out some details but at least they had passed through the inner circle of hell. He shifted onto his haunches and turned to look through the porthole into the bomb bay. Something was not quite right; instead of the lines of empty bomb carriers he could make out a dark cylindrical form. He took the torch from the clip in his compartment and shone it through the small panel. Their 'cookie', four thousand pounds of joy and goodwill that should by now be shattered metal in a Frankfurt fire, was obstinately refusing to part company with them. 'We've got a hang up, Skipper, the cookie's still with us. Do you want to go round again?'

'No thank you, Bomb Aimer.' The pilot's reply was just sufficient to override the more succinct advice that was offered in a strong Australian accent, the second word of which was 'Off'. That would have been from either the Mid Upper Gunner, Sergeant Reg Hudson or the Wireless Operator, Flying Officer Billy Stewart. Robbie's money was on Reg.

'We could never prove we'd dropped it on the target anyway as we've used the photo flash,' concurred Robbie.

'I'll try to get jettison the bloody thing. It's bound to hit something useful.' The pilot was sounding a bit irritated now so Robbie knew better than to debate the point.

The fires had died away now as they departed the target area. The pilot focused firstly on getting out of the immediate vicinity of the burning city before reaching for the emergency jettison handle. This had the desired result and the Lancaster leapt skywards again as the cookie fell free into the darkness.

'Cookie's gone, Skipper,' Robbie announced, even though he knew that the rest of the crew would have felt the loss of two tons of high explosive with unbridled relief. Another torch lit check of the bomb bay confirmed that it was now empty, as was right and proper. He lay on his front again and stared through the Plexiglas, waiting for the flash of the cookie exploding. As it did so he could, for a split second, see the outlines of buildings around the point of impact. 'I think we hit something down there, looks like a factory or something.'

'Navigator to Bomb Aimer, I've marked it. I'll report it when we get back and see what they reckon.' Flying Officer Pete Hughes was precise, almost pedantic, and the crew valued that in the man to whom the task fell of knowing exactly where they were at all times.

The cookie appeared to have started a few small fires, but Robbie knew that these were a bonus. Its main purpose was to break open buildings for the incendiaries to burn, but at the very least it would have given the locals something to keep them busy.

The blinding blue-white light came from nowhere. Robbie's night vision disappeared and he heard Ron swear, which was a rarity for the unflappable pilot. More searchlights came on and instantly gripped the bomber. Ron threw the Lancaster on to its wing tips as he struggled to escape.

Instinctively, Robbie grabbed his parachute from its stowage and clipped it to his harness. Cumbersome it might be, but he wasn't expecting to have to move around the aircraft right now. Where there were searchlights, there was bound to be flak. Sure enough, a cacophony of light and sound surrounded them as every anti-aircraft weapon in this part of Germany, it seemed, tried to blow them to pieces. Ron was manouvering the aeroplane with increasing desperation, but to no avail. Robbie felt the Lancaster shudder as a shell hit them; he couldn't see where but from the shouts over the intercom and the orange glow now coming from the cockpit area he knew it wasn't good.

'Parachutes on, chaps, get yourselves out.' Ron sounded almost unnaturally calm now, the stress having left his voice despite the grave peril he must have perceived for him to order his crew to bail out.

Robbie didn't question the order, or even stop to think. The forces acting on his body were getting more powerful by the second and it took a feat of strength to unplug his oxygen tube and intercom lead, turn around and open the escape hatch on top of which he had been lying. Lifting the hatch clear and stowing it as best he could, the Bomb Aimer crawled to the gap and pulled himself through it.

The incredible force and icy blast of the airstream stunned Robbie for a few moments. He barely noticed the bomber, by now trailing flames, as it lumbered past him. He was fortunate not to collide with any part of it and quickly lost momentum in the drag of the passing air. The noise and turbulence subsided and he felt weightless in a void, suspended between the starlit sky and the ground. Frankfurt was still burning in the middle distance but the ground beneath him, blacked out, was invisible. The power of rational thought remained with him and he felt through his gloves for the 'D' ring of his parachute pack. A good few seconds had elapsed since he had left the aircraft, which he could see falling away in the distance, a comet of flames and sparks, so he considered he would be below the height of the bomber stream. He gave the ring a firm pull, feeling himself jerked very firmly and somewhat painfully upright as his canopy deployed.

Free of the rush of air he had felt as he had plummeted in free fall, he now felt an unworldly calm as he hung suspended beneath his parachute. Whilst concentrating on his bombsight, resolving the hung-up cookie and reacting to the sudden crisis in the flak-torn Lancaster, his training had carried him through. His brain had been too focused on his numerous tasks to recognise fear. Now he had nothing else on his mind other than his immediate future and he was frightened. Alone, cold, and thousands of feet above a hostile land, it was fair to say that he had been in better situations. Even so, as he saw a sudden eruption of flame nearby, assuming it was the end of his Lancaster, Robbie realised that things could have been far worse for him.

Robbie could hear the sound of other, luckier, bombers and their crews homeward bound. Over Frankfurt, he saw the war continuing to rage; searchlights still probing and the red, yellow and orange bursts of flak greedily seeking further victims. Closer, but still a few miles behind him, the isolated specks of the small fires his own cookie had conjured up glowed dimly in the dark whilst just off to his side was the burning wreckage of his aircraft. He felt relieved that the forecast winds should, this night, carry him further away from the scenes of devastation to which he had contributed. Robbie knew that he was still not guaranteed a friendly reception wherever he came down.

As his eyes adjusted to the darkness below him, Robbie saw black shapes start to form, the tiny straight-edged forms which would be buildings interspersed with larger irregular patches that must, he presumed, be forest and woodland. He hoped they weren't lakes, though he couldn't decide whether he would prefer to land in trees or in water as neither would be conducive to his continuing good health.

Closer to the ground now, Robbie saw that he was drifting, inevitably, in the breeze but judged that he was heading towards a lighter patch of land. A field, perhaps, he thought. At that moment, he couldn't have cared less if it contained a cantankerous bull; he would be prepared to take his chance. The patch seemed to expand around him as he approached. That was a good sign as it suggested he was on track to land in it, and indeed he did. The last few seconds brought an apparent acceleration as the ground rushed to meet him. The landing was far harder than he had anticipated and, to his intense annoyance, he felt a sharp pain in his ankle.

Robbie was dragged across the field by the canopy, still inflated in the breeze, until it snagged in a hedgerow. His ankle bouncing over the uneven ground did nothing to ease his discomfort or improve his humour. He came to a rest lying on his back in coarse grass. Releasing his parachute harness before the canopy and wind had chance to further their conspiracy to drag him across Germany, he sat up and took stock of his situation. He might have been waking from a nap in an English meadow, had it not been the middle of the night and had he not been cold, injured and scared stiff. Being dressed in the uniform of an enemy airman who had just been trying, with some degree of success it must be thought, to slaughter the local population, was not likely to restore a feeling of normality any time soon.

He heard movement around him and discern the hiss of exhalation. Warm breath condensed mistily in the night air. His eyes had adjusted to the dark now and he cautiously looked around. There were several shapes surrounding him, some moving slowly, others were stationary and seemed lower to the ground. Occasional groans and sighs emanated from them. One or two, perhaps more curious than their fellows, started drifting towards him. Robbie decided that, having apparently been spotted already, there was little point in trying to curl up in the grass and make himself inconspicuous, so he stood up. The nearer shapes, not expecting this, appeared startled and edged back. He could see more clearly now and, from the light and dark patterns he could just make out, it transpired that he had landed amid a herd of Friesian cows.

Robbie knew that the cows, whilst unarmed and therefore unable to take him prisoner themselves, could easily draw attention to him if they panicked. The locals would be all too aware that his Lancaster had crashed; it was hard for such occurrences to pass unnoticed except in remote areas. He could see his parachute canopy quite clearly, bunched up against the hedge that had interrupted its wind-borne progress. He took a tentative step towards it, wincing as he put his weight on his ankle. It bore his weight, albeit grudgingly, so he considered that it was intact, if twisted. He slowly hobbled towards the hedge, gathering the parachute in his arms. The canopy eventually, at his insistence, parted company with the hedge; he was left now with the problem of how to dispose of it.

A couple of the bolder cows had wandered behind him to see what he was up to. Still moving with great caution, wary of causing a stampede or a cacophony of mooing, either of which might give away his position, he bundled the harness, cords and canopy together and shoved the package as far as he could into the middle of the hedge, as near to the ground as he could manage. Having no further use for his flying helmet and Mae West he stuck those inside the hedge as well, hoping that in broad daylight it was as dense and substantial as it appeared now. He thought about discarding his flying jacket but decided against doing so as that would mean wandering around Nazi Germany in his blue RAF battle dress and, in any case, he was cold.

Robbie edged along the boundary of the field for a couple of hundred yards until he came to a wooden gate, which he managed to open without too much trouble. He wasn't sure that his ankle would have been too happy about climbing over it, so he considered that a blessing. Closing the gate, as he had had enough of the company of the cows, he found himself on a rough track running between two hedges.

At this moment, Robbie had not the faintest idea which way to go; he could not be certain, with the pilot's desperate and ultimately unsuccessful manoeuvring, which way the Lancaster was heading when it crashed. He looked up; despite the patchy cloud he could make out most of the Plough constellation, which gave him an indication of North. He chose the direction of the lane which took him in the more westerly direction and, still favouring his painful, ankle, started on what he hoped would be his walk home.

Robbie didn't manage to walk as far as he had hoped. After a quarter of a mile or so the track curved sharply to the right, leading into a farmyard. Despite moving quietly, he could not avoid coming to the attention of a dog, which loudly announced his presence. Unfortunately, the dog was not alone and a man's voice shouted *'Wehr'st dar?'* Robbie, who had learnt only rudimentary German, in case he ever found himself in this situation, knew enough to recognise that he was being asked who was there. He could not think of a sensible answer, so simply froze, but the enquirer backed up his question by shining a torch at Robbie. After a split second of stunned silence, he heard the unmistakable sound of a rifle bolt being slid home, accompanied by a shout of *'Tommi Flieger!'* and the order to raise his hands. He did so; his injured ankle would not allow him the luxury of running away and the metallic click of the rifle suggested that in a fight there would only be one winner and it would not be him.

Any hopes that he might have been challenged by a single German were dashed by his would-be captor shouting for back up: *'Kurt, Johann, komm' hier, mach' schnell!'* Kurt and Johann needed, it would seem, no further bidding; the farmhouse door crashed open and two figures ran out wielding what Robbie assumed, in what little light there was, to be firearms. These they pointed at Robbie with some determination. However, he could sense that his sudden and unexpected arrival into their lives had delivered the reality of war to them personally. As far as he could tell, all three men seemed somewhat elderly and one of them was considerably more portly than was normal in crack fighting troops.

Whilst Robbie might ordinarily have fancied his chances against the three older men in an athletics arena or even a pub fight, the fact that they were armed, whilst he wasn't, gave them an overwhelming advantage. None of them seemed to have an injured ankle either, he thought ruefully. The first soldier, who had seemingly drawn the short straw, gestured at Robbie to keep his hands high whilst telling his mate Kurt to search him. Kurt, lanky and grey-haired with a drooping moustache and a hang-dog expression, approached Robbie gingerly and searched the pockets of his flying jacket which were empty. He then yanked at the zipper and opened the sheepskin leather garment almost fearfully, as if expecting to be ambushed from within. Finding no firearm, he then proceeded to pat the pockets of Robbie's battle dress tunic, finding only a packet of cigarettes and box of matches. These he brandished triumphantly, evidently considering them the spoils of war. He seized them, Robbie recognising that he was unlikely to see them again. Kurt's somewhat rudimentary search completed, the first soldier, whose name had not been uttered by anyone else so remained anonymous, waved his rifle again at Robbie and ordered him *'In das Haus.'* Surrounded by his new-found friends, he was marched without further ceremony into the kitchen of the farmhouse.

Robbie's appearance in the farmyard had caused some inconvenience to Kurt and Johann, if the kitchen table was to be believed. Two bowls bearing a stew-like material sat steaming, with spoons still immersed. Hunks of grey-brown bread were cast carelessly aside. A black pot sat on a range cooker, possibly with more of the stew therein. Emboldened by the domestic environment, Robbie asked

'Have I interrupted your dinner?' This met with a sharp retort of *'Halt die Fressel!'* from the still-nameless first soldier. Although this phrase was not in Robbie's German vocabulary, it was clear that he was being told to shut up.

All three of his captors wore bland field grey uniforms and Robbie did not recognise any unit badges. He was alarmed, however, to see that they had the runes of the SS on their collars. From their apparent age and appearance, he considered that they might well be from a reserve unit; they were far from the tall, young, blond caricatures the Nazis had shown off to an incredulous world before the war. Kurt said something to the first soldier, appearing to address him as Willi, so that made matters microscopically clearer. Willi went out of the kitchen into another part of the house, and the sound of a monologue soon became apparent. Robbie wondered if this house was blessed with a telephone, in which case it would make sense to use it as a de facto headquarters for the trio.

The kitchen door opened and a large woman, red-faced with straggly fair hair, bustled in. She asked, so far as Robbie could make out, what was going on and who on Earth this stranger was. Johann tried to persuade her to leave but it was clearly her kitchen and she would not be told what to do in her own home. She peered at Robbie, who now felt as disheveled as he must have looked, having come very close to being dragged, quite literally, through a hedge backwards. Pointing first to the stew then to Robbie, she asked him *'Werden Sie essen?'* Before his guards had a chance to express an alternative point of view, he nodded eagerly, replying, *'Ja, bitte.'* He hadn't felt any hunger until that point, but was mindful of the military adage to make the most of any such opportunity as there was no way of knowing when it would arise again. Within thirty seconds, he was sitting at the table of the German farmhouse eating a meal that was originally intended for a German soldier. This small victory gave him immense satisfaction.

He had finished the bowl and a hunk of bread by the time Willi returned. This was fortunate as it appeared that the German was not best pleased that his prisoner had been treated so kindly. On entering the kitchen, the soldier shouted at all and sundry, gesticulating at the woman and, for good measure, punching Robbie on the side of the head. Though the blow struck home, his ear smarting and ringing, Robbie managed to ride the shock and pain of the sudden attack and, for now, the assault ended there.

In his haste Willi had left the door open and Robbie saw that it led to a darkened hallway, with a set of stairs across the passage. For a moment, Robbie thought he saw a small girl peering through the posts. She was staring at him with intense curiosity but, at the same time, looking fearful, perhaps of incurring the wrath of her parents. About four or five years old, she had dark hair with a single curl in the middle of her forehead. For some reason, even though she was indoors she seemed to be wearing a thick coat. Robbie looked away momentarily and, when he looked again, the girl was no longer there.

Willi seemed to be the senior soldier there and he dished out orders to his colleagues, the woman and Robbie. Despite his swollen ear, Robbie still pretended not to understand German, and neither Kurt nor Johann seemed to have picked up on his ability to speak enough of their language to have tapped the woman up for a free tea. Naturally, this wound Willi up even further, which was Robbie's intent, though he knew he had to be careful lest he push his luck too far. An hour and a half later, by the kitchen clock, he heard a lorry pull up in the farmyard, accompanied by a copious amount of banging, crashing and shouting. So far, thought Robbie, the Wehrmacht was living up to its billing for bombastic and loutish behaviour.

The door to the yard opened and two more armed soldiers entered with a clear sense of purpose, accompanied by a third who looked, by his dress and bearing, like an officer. More shouting ensued, though this time it was all directed at Robbie. A couple more punches to the head by Willi were probably intended to impress the officer as well as to remind Robbie not to eat someone else's dinner; to the recipient it wholly academic. He was dragged to his feet and bundled outside into the farmyard. A lorry awaited, its metal cab followed wherever it went by a canvas-covered back. This, Robbie presumed, was his transport to wherever his captors planned to take him next. Before he could board the vehicle, the officer said something to his guards and he was thrown to the ground. The following moments, most likely a couple of minutes but seemingly endless to Robbie, passed in a torrent of kicks to his body. These he could endure; what he feared was being worked over by rifle butts. Under the circumstances Robbie knew that there was no point in complaining; no one would listen and any injuries would be explained away as having been sustained in his recent escape from a crashed aircraft. One or two kicks did catch his bruised ankle, the intense pain little short of agonising. Eventually the cream of the SS got bored with duffing up their prisoner. The officer shouted *'Aufstehen!'* and, following a final kick for luck, *'In das Wagen!'*

Robbie managed to regain his feet. With his hands and forearms, he had protected his head and face, but at the expense of what he knew would be bruises and abrasions the length of his body. From the nature of his working over and its relatively short duration, he considered that the kicking had been simply a warning against any thought of escaping. If the Germans had wanted they could have shot him out of hand and no one would have ever been the wiser.

It seemed that the young girl had followed Robbie from the house and he could see her, still staring at him, from the shadows near the back door. She had done him no harm and he bore her no ill, so he avoided paying attention to her, in case she was subsequently reprimanded. He allowed his guards to shove him up into the back of the lorry where he lay on the flat boards whilst the troops made themselves what passed for comfortable on the bench seats. The occasional poke in the ribs from a boot cap reminded him to lie still.

With a crashing of gears and rasp of its elderly engine, the lorry lurched unwillingly into motion. The uneven track they were evidently navigating did nothing to ease Robbie's discomfort, the jolts and jars passing effortlessly through the vehicle to home in on his aching and bruised body. He didn't bother trying to work out which way he was heading, though it was unlikely that they would be dropping him off at the Swiss border. In fact the trip was relatively short, twenty minutes or so, and then he was dragged unceremoniously out the lorry, accompanied by a few more cuffs to the head and body and plenty of enthusiastic shouting.

The lorry was now in an enclosed yard, though it was too dark for Robbie to see much in the way of detail. Two of his captors, probably Kurt and Johann who were at the bottom of the food chain, took an arm each and frog marched him into a dank and miserable building. A light bulb made a feeble attempt at illumination, but the peeling green paint and lack of interesting features probably made it wonder why it bothered. He did not get much time to see anything more, though, as the guards pushed him into a cell, slamming the door behind him with a resounding crash. A key turned and Robbie was left to himself.

The only light was that which filtered through a small aperture set high up in the wall and wholly out of reach. Robbie could make out a solid bench, upon which lay what looked like a mattress. He reached out and the rough cloth confirmed it to be so; a mattress indeed, albeit a very lumpy one. For want of any more meaningful activity, Robbie eased himself on to the makeshift bed and thought about his new lot in life. The only positive thought he could fix on was that he was still breathing.

At some point, Robbie dropped off, to be awoken an indeterminate time later by his cell door opening. The interior was not markedly brighter but at least it was merely gloomy rather than dark. In comparison, the green corridor beyond appeared to be brightly illuminated, though no more inspiring than before. Two guards, different from before, entered the cell. One ordered him, *'Komm!'* which was straightforward enough. Robbie swung his legs off the bed and eased himself to his feet. It was easier to identify the parts that didn't ache than those that did, but everything did still appear to be connected. His ankle bore his weight, if somewhat reluctantly. Holding his hands away from his body to show that he was not hiding anything, Robbie hoped to avoid a repeat of the beatings he had endured earlier.

The guards appeared more like policemen than soldiers, though both were carrying pistols. His main concern now was that he might be handed over to the Gestapo, a prospect that did not fill him with unbridled joy. However, when he was escorted into a small room containing a table and a couple of chairs, he was relieved to see that the man apparently awaiting his arrival wore a Luftwaffe uniform.

'Good morning and perhaps you will not think it amiss if I welcome you to Germany,' his new host greeted him. The man spoke with precise, almost clipped, words, far from the stereotypical tones Robbie had been expecting. Acutely conscious of the instruction drummed into him to give away nothing other than his name, rank and number, he still could not help himself returning the greeting with a mumbled 'Good morning.'

Perhaps already well versed in the niceties of the Geneva Convention, the Luftwaffe man continued, 'You and I know that you are allowed to introduce yourself, even if it is to a limited extent.'

'Robert Ticknall, Flying Officer, 1819612,' Robbie replied.

'Thank you, that was, I think, the easy bit. I am Oberleutnant Ziehm of the Luftwaffe Security Branch. I will shortly be escorting you to the reception centre we have for aircrew.' Robbie was hugely relieved to have been handed over to the Luftwaffe, rather than the Gestapo, and it meant that he had, for the present, parted company with the thugs of the SS. The intelligence briefings led him to be believe that they were less cruel than their counterparts, though they were, of course, still the enemy. His captor went on, 'When and where did your aeroplane crash?'

Robbie remained silent and looked at the officer who, after a somewhat prolonged pause, continued, 'Flying Officer Ticknall, please do not think I am here to interrogate you; you will go through that later. I simply need to ascertain that you are a member of the Royal Air Force and are here because we have shot down your aeroplane. We would not want people thinking that you were a spy after all. Please show me your identification tags.'

After a moment searching under his flying jacket and battle dress blouse, Robbie retrieved the two dog tags on their chain. He had to unzip his bulky flying jacket to do so. Without removing them, he held them as far forward as possible. Ziehm looked at them and was apparently satisfied. 'Thank you, Flying Officer Ticknall. That makes both our lives a little bit easier. Now, perhaps you could tell me where you were shot down?' Robbie smiled and shook his head.

'No matter. Perhaps I can help you. Shortly before you were captured by my rather heavy-handed colleagues, for which I feel I must apologise, by the way, a Lancaster crashed four kilometers away, or thereabouts. Your Lancaster, perhaps?' No reply.

'The wreckage will be fully examined later but the first report says that six bodies have been recovered, not seven, as one might expect.' Robbie again kept quiet but the news, if correct, that his crew mates had perished, was a hammer blow.

'We have found two air gunners, one wireless operator, one navigator, the pilot and the flight engineer, but not the bomb aimer. Tell me, Flying Officer Ticknall, what was your role in the crew?' Robbie looked at Ziehm, still not speaking, hoping that his face would give nothing away.

'If you will excuse me, Flying Officer Ticknall...' Ziehm leant forward and pulled the lapel of Robbie's jacket aside, exposing the half-winged brevet on his blouse. 'B. Bomb Aimer, Flying Officer Ticknall. This is a coincidence, is it not?' Ziehm sat back in his chair, clasping his hands behind his head in an overly-relaxed manner. 'I understand you feel that you must abide by the Geneva Convention. We were given precisely the same orders ourselves.' Robbie picked up the inference which did not go unnoticed by Ziehm. 'Yes, I am a flier too. Or rather, I was until I suffered a perforated ear drum which means, regrettably, that I must remain on the ground. I do understand your reluctance to talk. If we are to have a monologue, perhaps I should tell you what I know. You are a Bomb Aimer attached to 83 Squadron. Your Lancaster, a Mark One by the way, serial number ED265, took off from Royal Air Force Station Harmsfield Wold at approximately 1730 hours last night. Your target was the railway station in the centre of Frankfurt. At least, that is where your target markers fell so it is a fair presumption, is it not?' In the continuing absence of any comment by Robbie, Ziehm carried on, 'Whilst the raid continued, there was a single bomb explosion some distance from Frankfurt, dropped by a Lancaster that was possibly off course. Maybe your navigator was having a difficult day if he could not find Frankfurt...?' Ziehm raised his eyebrows.

The Luftwaffe kept meticulous records, that much Robbie knew, but even so the efficiency with which they had identified the aircraft, cross-checked the serial number and relayed this snippet of information to Ziehm surprised Robbie. He was in little doubt that there would be further such nuggets fed to him in his forthcoming interrogation.

'A cup of coffee, Flying Officer?' Robbie looked up and nodded. 'Yes please.'

Ziehm stood up and walked to the door. Opening it he called to an unseen orderly, '*Zwei Kaffee, bitte.*' Ziehm's courtesy seemed to extend to all around him and Robbie felt himself warming to the man. He cautioned himself, though, that the pleasantries following on from his earlier, more brutal, treatment, might simply be part of a 'Good cop, bad cop' routine.

The coffee arrived, the two mugs borne by an elderly man clad in the ubiquitous grey uniform. He placed them on the table and Ziehm invited Robbie, 'Please, you choose one and I will drink it. This is not a trick, but like all fliers I am accustomed to having a cup of coffee on the rare occasions it is offered. Again, I must apologise though, it is, as you would put it, bloody horrible. There is a war on, you know...'

Handing one mug to Ziehm, who drank from it, Robbie then sipped his own. Lukewarm and bitter, at least it gave him a slight sense of normality. Ziehm changed tack. 'Do you mind if we are, perhaps, a little less formal? We are, after all, both fliers. I am Martin, which is also, I think, an

English name. And you are...?' The question hung for a moment or two, until Robbie relented. 'Robbie.'

'Like the poet, then, Burns,' Ziehm commented.

'You speak good English,' Robbie acknowledged.

'In better times, my father was an engineer. Machine tools, not aeroplanes or their engines, I would hasten to add. He travelled to England quite often and said English was the language of the future. That is not a popular idea nowadays but no matter. We had holidays too. Margate,' Ziehm added.

'I have to say I have never been there,' Robbie responded, though not wishing to sound churlish. 'I would prefer to be there right now though, as I'm sure you'd understand.'

'I was in London for a year as well.' Ziehm was warming to the theme of his own life story, though Robbie did wonder how much was fabricated as part of an elaborate act to elicit details from him. 'My father secured from a good contact an engineering apprenticeship for me. He thought it would be useful for me to have a trade in case I went to university but failed in my studies. He did not have a high opinion of my academic abilities.' Ziehm drank some more of his coffee. 'And now we are sworn enemies. The best laid plans of mice and men, as the other Robbie would say.' Ziehm stood up. 'Please finish your coffee, Robbie. We have to leave now and there is something I need to show you.'

Ziehm called the orderly, speaking briefly to him and remaining standing as the man stomped lethargically away along the corridor. 'We should respect some formalities, Robbie. My colleagues, whom you will meet in a minute, are armed, and I am also armed. Despite our courtesies I am afraid I will have no alternative but to shoot you, should you decide to escape. You would also find that escaping airmen are not made welcome either by the Gestapo or the civilian population. Whilst you are with the Luftwaffe that is as good as it gets. Please do not push your luck.'

Ziehm's colleagues also wore Luftwaffe insignia and, if not warm and friendly, had treated him with courtesy. As they escorted him out of the building he noted that their hands rarely strayed far from the holsters containing their sidearms. A large grey Mercedes saloon car, its front wing bearing a Luftwaffe flag, awaited the group. Its driver already had the engine running and sat impassively while Robbie was assisted into the rear of the car, sandwiched between the two escorts. Ziehm, by all accounts the ranking officer amongst the entourage, eased himself into the front passenger seat where he had a brief muttered conversation with the driver. His directions apparently made clear and understood, he turned around in the seat so he could continue to address Robbie. The car pulled out of the yard and left behind them what appeared to be the police station of a small town. By now Ziehm had established himself as a master of small talk, pointing out to Robbie various landmarks and points of interest, though his comments, perhaps by design, never actually told Robbie anything of value.

Eventually the driver left the main road and eased the car along a tree-lined lane. 'First, I have a certain duty to carry out, and it is also important for you,' Ziehm informed him. 'It will not be pleasant but it is necessary.' The latter comment did nothing to cheer Robbie up and his heart sank further as the car pulled up alongside a field gate.

Ziehm alighted first and opened the rear door for Robbie and his guards. 'We will get out now for a short while, but I must remind you not to try anything. We have sidearms but our driver has a sniper rifle and is trained in its use. I am certain I can rely on your common sense but I do not wish to stake my career on it.' He turned away and led the way to the gate, holding it open for the group to pass through. Far from being pinioned, Robbie was afforded some space by the escort. He realised that they were simply giving him a gap of a few feet. He could not hope to tackle more than a single guard whilst the rest would have ample time and space to shoot him should they feel so inclined.

They emerged from the tree line which had been sufficiently dense to shield from their view the wreckage of a Lancaster. Whilst there had clearly been a fire, the bent and torn metal was not burnt out. A small number of soldiers were posted individually around what remained of the aircraft. It was, Robbie was grieved to see, the Lancaster from which he had baled out a few hours previously. Worse, there was a large tarpaulin draped over six shapes on the ground next to what had been the cockpit. Robbie did not need a vivid imagination to realise that the shapes were his crewmates.

Following a short conversation with Ziehm, the soldier who was, Robbie assumed, the NCO in charge of the detail told two of the sentries to remove the cover. As he had expected, Robbie found himself looking at the bodies of his crew. He didn't need to say anything; Ziehm saw the reaction he had been looking for. 'Your aeroplane and your comrades, Robbie. I am sorry that you go through this.'

'Martin.' Robbie was feeling his composure start to crack as he faced reality. 'Please will you ensure that they are treated with respect?'

'Of course. We are not savages, Robbie. I think now we have seen enough. We must continue our journey.'

Robbie turned away. He heard the tarpaulin rustle as the sentries replaced it over his mates. His emotions were mixed. He was desperately sorry for the deaths of his friends; like most bomber crews they had become as close as brothers. At the same time, he felt the relief and the guilt of having survived. It had simply been his good fortune that his crew position was directly on top of the escape hatch and that he had clipped on his parachute while he had chance.

'Thirty-seven bombing operations for your aeroplane. Not so many for you, I think. We know they take you away from your ops when you reach thirty.' Ziehm was walking closer to Robbie now, though still ensuring there was a gap to allow him to react. 'You know the Luftwaffe does not embrace such a concept. You fly until you can fly no more. Perhaps the staff believe that the war will end soon. That is what they are told.' He glanced around, almost furtively, to check that his colleagues were out of earshot. 'You and I know differently, Robbie. You send seven hundred, perhaps eight hundred bombers in a night. We shoot down, usually twenty, sometimes more and sometimes less. Your factories build Lancasters faster than we shoot them down and every month ships bring hundreds or maybe thousands of aircrew from your Empire. We know they come from

Canada, from Australia, New Zealand, even Jamaica I think. That is at night. In the day, it is the Americans. And our staff now must think, 'Do we send the Luftwaffe's fighters and flak batteries to fight the Russians or do we keep them at home?' Even Herr Goering cannot pretend to be in two places at once. I think perhaps Mr. Churchill and your 'Butch' Harris know this when they tell you to come and bomb our towns and cities. It suits Stalin for two reasons to have you do this. Firstly, it makes it easier for his troops to push us back and secondly it means that you will already have broken Germany so he will not have to. Perhaps, as aircrew, you will have noticed that mostly you attack Western Germany. The East of Germany is not so easy for you. Harris gave up on Berlin. There is not so much industrial damage in the East, like I say, and perhaps that suits Stalin also as he is attacking from that direction.' They were approaching the car now. Ziehm sighed. 'Perhaps for you it is academic. I sincerely hope your part in the war is over. One day, you will be allowed to return to your family. The soldier who captured you, though, he will not be.' Ziehm's voice tailed off. Robbie glanced at him, waiting for the answer to his own unspoken question. Ziehm continued, 'His family lived in Hamburg until July this year. The RAF bombed it for three days. His wife, children, parents, they were all killed. You were fortunate that the bounty for capturing an airman was money his colleagues needed, otherwise I think...' Ziehm made a pistol gesture and left the rest to Robbie's imagination.

The journey continued for a while in silence. After half an hour or so the main road led to the outskirts of what Robbie presumed was Frankfurt. There were few signs of the war initially, other than the prevalence of uniforms and the overall look of weariness on the faces of the population. There were, at first, one or two damaged buildings, appearing at random. The unintended targets of stray bombs, there was no pattern to their selection. As the car made its way towards the city centre, though, the wreckage became more widespread, encompassing rows of houses, apartment blocks and a few factories. Ziehm turned to one of Robbie's escorts and spoke briefly. The guard uttered a confirmatory *'Ja'* and handed Robbie his cap.

'I suggest you put that on,' Ziehm said. Robbie looked at the proffered cap, then at Ziehm, asking him, 'Why?'

'This is Frankfurt. Last night you, and I do mean you personally, bombed the city. I do not know how many people were killed exactly but there were many. These people,' Ziehm waved his hand in the general direction of the population, 'do not know and would not care. They would just hang you from a streetlight. It is perhaps best that you do not draw attention to yourself.' Accepting the logic of Ziehm's argument, Robbie put on the cap and slumped down in the seat, as if using a routine car journey to catch up on much-needed sleep.

As they progressed the devastation became more apparent and the damage more recent. Ruined buildings abounded, many smouldering, some still with flames slowly consuming the remaining timbers. Robbie tried to identify factories and public buildings but wherever he looked, he saw mostly houses and apartment blocks.

Rubble blocked the side streets, in some places it had been moved partly aside to allow the passage of people and small carts, in others left to form a barrier that must be scrambled over. Here and there buildings were miraculously intact, the random selection for destruction having left them unscathed, though there was precious little glass unbroken in these either. Makeshift signs adorned doorways and window spaces, marking the remnants of a lost world. It was the people, though, who moved Robbie most. Clad in the odds and sods of whatever garments they could lay their hands on, forlorn beings shambled aimlessly amongst the detritus of their homes. Undead in the sense that their existence bore no reality to their former life these drifting spirits haunted the places in which they had lived and loved.

More ruins lay aside the road as the car crept tortuously towards the centre of Frankfurt, these even more recent if the activity around them was a guide. More purposeful groups worked on the smoking piles of bricks and wood, here and there amidst pools of water from burst mains. Robbie guessed that this was the result of the previous night's endeavours.

Still forms were lined up next to some destroyed buildings, what remained of their decency protected by blankets, curtains or even just coats. Some were the size of adults, others smaller. These were the victims, realised Robbie. 'Bombs gone..!' had led to this; women and children, some of them dead by his own hand.

Robbie saw her then, the girl from the farm, still in her dark coat. She was standing alone next to a body which was shrouded with cloth. Looking at him, her eyes followed the progress of the car as it passed where she stood, a sentinel to the departed. He averted his eyes for a moment or two and when he looked back she was gone.

Robbie could only imagine that her parents must be involved in the rescue effort. In the world they now inhabited, perhaps even the children were accustomed to the results of total war.

'Women and children, Flying Officer Ticknall,' Ziehm commented from the front seat. 'And you wonder why they call you *terrorfliegers*.' Robbie did not feel that Ziehm expected a reply, so did not offer one.

The remainder of the car journey passed in silence. Robbie speculated that Ziehm might have played a good hand. After his initial rough treatment, along came the courteous and civilised fellow airman, engaging him in harmless small talk before shocking him with the sight of his colleagues' bodies. After the softening up came the hard word, bringing home to the Bomb Aimer the outcome of his efforts. Dead by his hand.

Robbie and Ziehm parted company when they arrived a brief time later at what the German told him was a Luftwaffe interrogation centre. Ziehm, whether or not the devious manipulator of Robbie's conscience, seemed to bear him no ill will.

'I hardly need say that if you behave properly the Luftwaffe will treat you in the same way,' were Ziehm's closing sentiments. 'It is, perhaps, not proper that we should be seen to shake hands, but perhaps one day we will meet again and, as you English like to say, we will laugh about all this.' Robbie thought that was highly unlikely but did Ziehm the courtesy of saluting, which was returned.

The interrogation process, whilst thorough, was not as brutal as Robbie had feared. It was, not unnaturally, prolonged by his unwillingness to tell the Germans anything useful. After a few days of stating nothing other than his name, rank and number, he was starting to get bored. His interrogators had, occasionally, given him pieces of information about his squadron that they had acquired elsewhere so he amused himself for a while feeding back various snippets to other inquisitors when they came to question him. It didn't take Robbie long to start embellishing these with spurious details that he dreamt up in the long hours in his cell. He conjured up a range of different airfields to which his squadron was considering moving, including the Scilly Isles from where, he assured a fascinated young officer, the Lancasters would be able to bomb Madrid. This was, he continued, a necessary prelude to the forthcoming invasion of Spain which would be launched through Gibraltar.

After Robbie had spent two days trying to persuade the Luftwaffe's intelligence staff that the Lancaster's Merlin engines had been converted to run on cold tea, the Germans eventually concluded that there was little benefit in interrogating him further. The following day he was put in the back of a lorry with two guards in whose company he was taken to a railway station. The next leg was by train to a prisoner of war camp, two slow and tedious days to the East. The only redeeming feature of the journey was that the Luftwaffe apparently considered its prisoners worthy of second class travel, with a compartment solely occupied by the three air force men.

The second night on the train was when Robbie next saw the young girl. Half-awake, he was drowsily watching his guards engrossed in one of their interminable rounds of cards when he became aware of a movement in his peripheral vision. Through the internal window to the corridor he saw her standing silently watching him. She was still dressed exactly as before though this did not surprise Robbie as much as the fact that she appeared to be heading East with him. He could see her face clearly for the first time; pale and gaunt she looked in need of a wholesome meal, which was at odds with the well-fed countenance of the woman at the farm, whom he presumed to have been the child's mother. The girl looked disconsolate but beyond the stage where crying achieved anything worthwhile. As he watched, she reached towards him as if wanting him to take her hand. And then she faded from view.

An intense shiver ran down Robbie's spine. His guards had not taken their eyes off the cards so he presumed that they had not seen anything untoward. Wide awake now, Robbie stared back into the corridor but the girl did not reappear. He eventually persuaded himself that he had been dreaming. He was, after all, a trained and disciplined combatant, but stress and fatigue could easily, he knew, conspire to cause him to hallucinate. The young girl was no more likely to be stalking him on this train across Germany than she was to be haunting him from beyond the grave. Satisfied, eventually, with his own explanation, Robbie fell into as deep a sleep as was possible under the circumstances.

The following eighteen months tested Robbie's boredom threshold to its limits, though it was an endurance that he could share with the two thousand or so other aircrew who found themselves in the same situation. Attempting to escape had been drummed into the camp's residents as their duty though it quickly became clear to Robbie that this was no more than an aspiration for most, rather than being in any way practical. For all their plans to dig tunnels, disguise themselves as local workers or hide themselves in vehicles, nothing came to fruition. As officers, they were spared a work detail so could not even use that as an opportunity to run away. The time passed exceedingly slowly, which gave Robbie plenty of time to dwell on his capture and what he had experienced immediately afterwards.

In training and on the squadron Robbie had not given much thought to the consequences of his bombing duties. Like all his comrades, he had been working hard to learn his new trade and to work within a highly disciplined organisation. He had never seriously considered the moral aspects of bombing. For a start, he thought it was not his place to question his orders which were, in any case, to take the war to the German heartland. Secondly, whenever the targets themselves were discussed, there was always a legitimate objective; industrial facilities they might be but each was directly or indirectly linked to the Nazi war effort. He was aware that the scale of the bombing extended beyond the boundaries of the factories themselves but the Luftwaffe had been no more careful in the Battle of Britain and the Blitz. Seeing his crew mates lying next to the shattered Lancaster had brought home his personal involvement in the air war, whilst the bodies of the civilians demonstrated all too clearly the indiscriminate carnage of total war.

Robbie's sympathy for the unwitting victims of strategic bombing took seed as a natural empathy with people who had, almost certainly, been uninvolved with the brutality surrounding them. Once in place, though, it was not easily uprooted. Boredom gave him too much time to think and dwelling on the innocent dead nurtured his concerns. As the weeks and months dragged on, his conscience was increasingly tormented by the thought that he might have been no better than a murderer.

He had been incarcerated for six months when he next saw her. Withdrawn into himself, he spent his days in introspection and his nights fighting off his demons. He was sitting on the step of the hut which served as accommodation for too many men. Robbie was looking through the two wire fences towards the pine forest beyond when he saw two small figures. He was sure they had not been there a few seconds previously and, for a moment, wondered how they had arrived unnoticed. Then he recognised the young girl, dressed exactly as before with her coat and hat. This time, though, she had brought with her a smaller child, a little boy with fair hair who stood alongside the girl, holding her hand. His short coat was scruffy and in need of repair. He wore light brown shorts beneath which a pair of undernourished legs made a valiant effort to hold him up. The girl pointed to Robbie, and said something to the boy who simply stared at him. Then they disappeared.

Having witnessed her previous vanishing act on the train, this no longer shocked Robbie; he was more mystified as to who she was and why she periodically appeared before him. His emotions had been ground down by his months of boredom, the lack of reliable news of progress towards freedom and the poor living standards he and his fellow captives had to endure. He also missed his mates on the crew, as well as his own family. Robbie carried a burden of guilt that he had survived when the rest of his crew had not. The knowledge that his role in the crew placed him directly on top of one of the few exits from an airborne Lancaster did nothing to assuage the feeling that some of his mates should have got out as well. It was no consolation to him that the situation had been totally out of his control and that he had had mere seconds to get out of the aircraft before it went into a terminal spin, pinning him helplessly within his compartment. Robbie was, at that time, unaware of the statistics that would later show the survival rate from a shot-down Lancaster to be one crewman in seven, exactly the proportion in his own case.

The apparition, Robbie thought, must have some reason for her focus on him. She had looked directly at him, reached towards him and, this time, pointed him out to her companion. But so far she had not made any attempt to contact him. Robbie wondered, again, if he was going around the bend. He did not consider that it was a good move just yet to mention his visions to his fellows; it was bad enough to be behind the wire for the indefinite future without their having to share the experience with a madman.

Robbie had reached the conclusion that if the girl was not a figment of his otherwise under-occupied imagination, then she must be a ghost, and probably a German one at that. He had never seen her before the night at the farm so, he reasoned, she must be local. In the few ghost stories he had read as a child none had mentioned spooks travelling abroad to haunt other countries. He wondered if she had died at the farm and had latched on to him out of boredom. More likely, and the thought made him very uneasy, was that she had been killed in an air raid. He had, after all, also seen her with the shrouded bodies in Frankfurt, watching him as he was driven past. The logical progression of his thoughts was to wonder if she had been killed by a bomb that he had dropped. That would explain her following him, he concluded, the notion causing him to shudder as a chill ran the length of his spine.

Even this most unlikely explanation for what might just be a figment of his imagination did nothing to account for the appearance of the young boy, who had been nowhere to be seen during the girl's previous manifestations. Once again Robbie wracked his brain for any similar occurrence in any of the tales he had read in his adolescence, but could find none. Writers of the paranormal evidently did not consider that phantoms were any more likely to bring their friends along on a haunting than they were to go on an afterlife holiday overseas.

The germ of the idea that he had been responsible for the girl's death took hold and began to spread through his conscience. Even if the apparition had an earthlier explanation Robbie was now acutely aware that, quite possibly, he had killed many people in the seventeen bombing raids he had undertaken before being obliged to attempt a return home on foot. He could see the girl as an individual human being, probably alive and well until some thirty seconds after he had pressed the bomb release button and dropped a thousand pounds of steel and amatol on her. It was no help whatsoever that she had, equally probably, been terrified when she heard the massed drone of seven hundred heavy bombers approaching, the whistle of descending bombs and the cacophony of explosions growing to a crescendo before the climax which had seen her blown to Kingdom come. Bombing aircraft factories, military facilities, even oil plants and the transport infrastructure had been justifiable, even reasonable, but slaughtering children had never actually entered his mind as something for which he was personally responsible. Now, Robbie felt, the girl was probably wanting to hold him to account. He could, for now, only speculate on how she might wish to do that.

The life of a POW was a matter of endless, dreary routine. Robbie did not keep tally of the days; he had no end date in sight and thought it most likely that one day he would either be killed or die of boredom. He realised that he could, had he so chosen, step over the trip wire a few feet inside the first of two fences. A warning shout, probably in German: *'Halt! Oder ich schiesse!'* before a mighty blow as the bullet struck him and brought oblivion. There were days when Robbie, in his growing misery, was sorely tempted to take that step. It was on such days that he mainly saw his personal ghosts; invariably the girl would appear when he was feeling particularly low, sometimes by herself but increasingly the small boy, probably her brother or perhaps a friend, would be with her. They would look directly at him; on the occasions when he was in a group she would point him out to the little lad who would invariably stare curiously at him. When Robbie was in a group, no one else seemed to notice them, and Robbie never pointed them out.

Robbie felt a growing urge to speak to the girl, notwithstanding the likely language difficulties, but there was always the physical barrier of the two fences and the killing zone. He realised that it had ever been thus; he had seen her through the compartment window on the train, the car window in Frankfurt and even in the farmhouse she had been out of reach. Thinking back, once again, to those earlier stories, he could not remember any in which ghosts and the living ever directly conversed. Maybe, he thought, it was something that neither entity had actually tried.

Any suggestion that the bombing of enemy cities was other than a strategic necessity would, not unnaturally, have been considered anathema to Robbie's fellow captives. Defeatist talk was not conducive to maintaining what little morale was still available to the prisoners and, he knew, would be swiftly dealt with. At the back of their minds was the possibly that some of their number might somehow be turned by the Germans, and to be considered a 'stool pigeon' would not be good for anyone's health. So, Robbie continued to keep his own counsel, morosely sitting and struggling with his demons.

Eventually his burden became too much to bear. The final straw came around what passed in the camp for Christmas in 1944. There were two final nails rather than one and these, for Robbie, closed the coffin lid firmly on his emotional well-being. A camp guard told him, in his moderately proficient English, that the Wehrmacht forces had launched an astonishingly successful counter-offensive in Belgium. It was only a matter of time, he said, before Antwerp fell back into Nazi hands, cutting the supply lines of the Allied ground forces. The Fuehrer had, *natürlich*, planned this all along having strategically pulled his forces back to stretch the Tommies and Amis ever since they had landed in Normandy.

Later the same day a new prisoner arrived in the camp, an Australian air gunner who had been shot down and evaded for a while prior to his capture. In conversation with his new comrades, the Aussie related how two of his crew mates had been rounded up and summarily shot dead by an SS soldier. He had subsequently learned from the Dutch Resistance people sheltering him that all captured Allied air crew were to be shot as war criminals, on the direct orders of Hitler. The local family in whose house he had been found were taken away in a truck to face an uncertain future which was almost certain to end cruelly. The Aussie found himself a guest of the Gestapo, whose personnel made him feel extremely unwelcome. After a couple of weeks languishing in a dank and dismal cell, being threatened constantly with torture and execution, he was unceremoniously despatched to Buchenwald concentration camp where, he told Robbie and his mates, was to be found hell on Earth. The inmates, mostly German, were little more than skin and bone, rations virtually non-existent and the squalid accommodation made their own camp appear luxurious in comparison. What sickened Robbie most was the Aussie's assertion that death amongst the inmates was apparently seen by the guards and camp officials as something to be encouraged at every opportunity, with a helping hand wherever they felt necessary. The Aussie gunner only secured a transfer when he had a chance encounter with a visiting delegation from Berlin. The members included two Luftwaffe officers, who were clearly unhappy with what they saw. He insisted on surrendering to them in person. This they apparently seized as a chance to make an honourable exit from an exceptionally dishonourable situation, taking their new-found prisoner with them.

Robbie was suddenly overcome by a wave of the blackest depression. The prisoners were vaguely aware of the ground offensives in the West as well as the East, as the news was updated by each new inmate. If the Allies were driven back, Robbie could foresee the war continuing for years or even resulting in a German victory. The Nazis' cavalier disregard for the life even of their own people did not bode well for those they already branded war criminals. It would surely not be long before the authorities decided that dead prisoners would be cheaper and easier to keep than live ones, and took steps to exterminate them all. They would probably consider that, by claiming they were 'war criminals', the outcry would be kept to a minimum.

He could see no way out. Accepting that the girl had made her point and led him to draw his own conclusion, he decided that he had had enough. Without speaking further, he stood, mumbling indistinctly about stretching his legs. He wanted no one to prevent him now that he had made the decision he realised had been at the back of his mind for a while. No one reacted as he walked slowly towards the trip wire. Even as he stood a foot or so short of it, no one thought there was anything amiss. One more step, Robbie thought as he contemplated the thin strip, and all that would change. A shout, in German but very clear in its message. Then a further step and blissful oblivion, assuming whichever guard challenged him was neither a poor shot nor a sadist. Knowing that blissful peace would come so quickly, along with freedom from the burden of guilt that he had carried since his day in Frankfurt, did not make it easy to step over the wire. His sense of self-preservation was still within him and Robbie chided himself for his weakness when he needed to be strong. He raised his eyes to focus on the open land beyond the barbed wire, wanting to see freedom as he died even if he could not reach it.

He saw the children standing by the second fence. They were, as before, watching him. The girl spoke to the boy, who seemed to Robbie more worried than curious. He clutched her arm and stared fearfully at Robbie. If anything, their appearance put steel in his resolve. He would simply walk towards them; if they were indeed ghosts he hoped that they would treat him sympathetically when he reached the other side of whatever great divide he was about to cross. As he lifted his foot the girl looked startled, then horrified. She lifted her hand as if to push him back, and mouthed what he interpreted as *'No…no!'* while the young lad buried his face in her coat.

Robbie paused, one foot held momentarily in mid-air before lowering it back to the ground, on the safe side of the trip wire. The small boy now looked at Robbie once more, tears streaming down his face. Robbie still wanted to go to them and took half a step towards the wire once more. This time he could swear he heard the girl as she mouthed the same words. He realised she was shouting *'Nein…nein!'* in her own language, though it made no difference to the meaning. It was apparent even in Robbie's tormented mind that she did not want him to cross the line. For a second time, he backed down. Still standing short of the trip wire he looked through the fences at the children, seeing to his renewed surprise that they were no longer alone. Misty figures gradually materialised, vague and ethereal at first, their forms slowly becoming more opaque and taking on form as they gained substance. Most of them were clad in grubby pyjama-like clothing, striped blue and grey. The few became ten, then twenty and more. The ghostly figures clustered around the children, the crowd growing into the hundreds and then thousands until it filled the open ground between the outer fence and the forest. Robbie could still hear the murmur of voices, this time from the throng rather than just the two children. As the sound grew in volume, he could hear it was the repetition of two words: *'Vergiss uns nicht.'* Don't forget us.

There was no way now that Robbie was going to cross the wire. It was abundantly clear that the girl, boy and, by implication, all their ghostly friends, wanted him to stay this side of the trip wire, and therefore alive. He took an exaggerated step backwards to show the phantom audience that he had got the message. The crowd then slowly faded from view, the volume of their voices diminishing as they dissolved into nothing. For good measure, he waved to the children who remained in view. The girl smiled and the little boy waved back. Then they, too, vanished. Suddenly aware of where he was, Robbie looked round. None of his fellow prisoners seemed to have seen anything out of place.

The episode was a tipping point for Robbie. He believed that the children, and those who appeared with them, were well-disposed towards him, but that they did not want him to join them yet. He must yet have a purpose to serve, though it had yet to make itself clear to him. This in turn shook him out of his self-imposed misery and extreme introspection, his natural good humour emerging from the hibernation it had endured since he was shot down.

He didn't see the ghosts again during the remainder of his incarceration. He realised that they had only appeared to him when he was at his lowest ebb, so wrote them off as a psychological or emotional defence mechanism. Whatever the cause, Robbie was grateful to his own mind for preventing him doing something stupid.

Liberation, when it came, was something of an anti-climax after the initial excitement of truckloads of GIs arriving one afternoon, shortly after the German guards had staged a walk-out, leaving their weapons behind. The previously-loquacious guard, so convinced that the Nazis were about to fight the Allies back to the English Channel, had recently started muttering darkly about the approaching *'Russen'* of the Red Army. Robbie presumed that they were hell-bent on surrendering to the US Army and didn't want any trigger-happy American troops to find them armed and shoot them just in case. Robbie thought he would have enjoyed the irony.

There was no real rush on the part of the Allied Occupying Powers to return Robbie to the UK. He was shipped back to Frankfurt, of all places, and housed in a former Wehrmacht barracks while he waited his turn to be repatriated. Finding himself once again with plenty of time on his hands he negotiated with a local US Army unit to borrow a jeep and a tank of petrol, explaining to the casually uninterested GI that he needed to carry out a local search for downed RAF aircraft. The American simply said 'Sure, Bud' and told him where to obtain petrol against a signature. The bill should be sent to the RAF, Robbie asserted. He doubted it would ever catch up with him and if it did, they could take it out of his back pay, accrued whilst he was in the POW camp.

His intention, at first, was simply to find and return to where his Lancaster had come down and then, he hoped, to locate the resting place of his mates. When he eventually returned to England he planned to visit their families and it would be of some limited comfort if he could tell them where they lay. He had, therefore, also borrowed a map of the area from his American friend. It mattered not that the legend was in German; he figured that he would simply navigate his way from village to village and hoped that eventually he would find the lane he had previously been driven down with Ziehm.

From his last flight, he knew that they had approached the target, the railway station in the city centre, from the south and had then turned on to a heading just north of due west. As far as he could remember, they had been shot down some ten minutes after bombing which at the three miles per minute achieved by the Lancaster into the headwind suggested that he would have been thirty miles from the city. That was in line with the road trip back to Frankfurt, he thought. Consulting his map, he decided to start his search around the small town of Breithardt. He could always ask the locals, he thought wryly. Despite the non-fraternisation policy still in place he could justify any such contacts as enquiries into the whereabouts of six missing aircrew and, come to that, one rather war-torn Avro Lancaster.

It transpired that the Germans he encountered were, in fact, unfailingly courteous and helpful. It appeared to Robbie that they were as glad as he to see the end of hostilities. They had to pick up their lives and move on, accepting that the uniforms might have changed but there was still a form of order, albeit of a far less brutal nature. He did not recognise any landmarks immediately but this did not particularly surprise him; the last time he had traced this path it was dark and he had been at twenty thousand feet, if relatively briefly.

Arriving in Breithardt in the middle of the morning he parked his jeep and found a café. Coffee was still in short supply but the grey haired and bearded owner provided a pot and cup. He was used to drinking it black after eighteen months as a prisoner and this coffee was a luxury compared with what he had endured for so long. The café was otherwise unoccupied so he asked the owner, *'Sprechen Sie Englisch?'* The answer appeared to be in the negative but the owner raised a finger and told Robbie, *'Bitte, warten.'* In no rush, Robbie was happy to wait. A few minutes later, the man re-appeared with a fair-haired woman, aged in her early twenties, in tow. *'Nina. Sie spricht Englisch,'* he announced to Robbie proudly.

Nina was, she told Robbie, the owner's daughter. She had studied English with a view to teaching it, but there had until recently been limited opportunities in that direction locally. Her understanding of, and ability to speak, English were more than adequate for Robbie's purposes, however. In answer to his questions, she could suggest three or four locations where she knew downed bombers had come to grief. Her knowledge of the area would be immensely useful if she could accompany him, Robbie thought, so broached the matter to Nina and, through her, to her father. There was a prolonged amount of intense discussion between the café owner and his daughter, together with much twirling of his beard by the older man, for whom this was apparently an indispensable aid to clear thought. Nina told Robbie that their concern was the Americans' strict rules on German civilians having anything to do with Allied military personnel. Privately, Robbie thought that this would be given only token lip service by the notoriously sex-starved GIs before being ignored completely in cases such as Nina, but he decided not to share that opinion. He agreed to take the woman to the local police station, now almost certainly an outpost of Uncle Sam's spreading empire, and complete the necessary paperwork that would see her registered as an interpreter for the Royal Air Force.

He drove through the town under Nina's direction and at once recognised the police station as the venue of his first overnight stay. This did not unduly surprise Robbie and it confirmed to him that he was in the right area. The necessary form-filling and permit-issuing was completed by an obviously sceptical and somewhat envious Master Sergeant, on the understanding that this was for short-term urgent and immediate enquiries only. They returned to the café, reassured the owner that his daughter was now an accredited attachment to His Majesty's Royal Air Force, even though the RAF itself was yet unaware of this, and set off to look for the crash site.

The first location Nina pointed out bore no resemblance to the field Robbie remembered. It was on the side of a steep hill in the middle of a wooded area, a transformation that even the Nazis could not have ordered, so he mentally struck that from the list. The second, however, was the right place. There was, by now, no sign of the events of that night. The Lancaster had long since been scooped up, taken away and its aluminium airframe melted down, presumably to fly again in the ultimately ironic form of a Luftwaffe night fighter. The field was now of long grass, which Nina said would be for hay to keep the livestock going over winter. Robbie found the indentations made by the Lancaster as it came to an enforced halt, but other than that no immediate trace remained. The striations across the field gave him the line on which the aircraft had made its final approach and the pair walked slowly through the grass. Patches of bare earth lay here and there, the soil perhaps still polluted by fuel or oil. In one such rut, some distance from where the wreckage had lain, Robbie saw a small glint of light. He knelt and, using a stone, scraped away at the surface layer. He found a battered wristwatch which he recognised as an official issue RAF chronometer. The strap was torn; Robbie realised that it must have been lost on impact. The watch still showed twenty-three minutes past eleven, which was about the time they crashed. There was no way of knowing to which of his friends the watch had been issued so Robbie considered it should remain in his own care on their behalf.

Nina told him that the airmen would usually have been buried in the nearest cemetery, so when they had finished their walk around the crash site, she took Robbie to a village church a couple of miles away. It was the work of minutes to identify six graves in a row in the churchyard.

Each was marked by a simple wooden cross bearing the airman's name, service number and date. Robbie was briefly seized by the notion that there might have been seven, contemplating the space at the end of the line which would, under less fortunate circumstances, have been his own resting place. He did not progress that chain of thought too far however, having travelled that route in the camp. He sat on the grass for a while, silently thinking of his mates. Nina quietly left him to his thoughts, walking off to another part of the churchyard. He appreciated the gesture. Eventually, still mentally miles away, he felt her hand on his arm. 'Your friends,' she said quietly. 'It was a terrible thing, the war. I lost my boyfriend and my brother. It is hard, especially for my father.'

'They were fighting, I suppose?' Robbie asked.

Nina noticed the fleeting look of wariness in Robbie's eyes. 'Yes. They were friends which is how I met Jürgen. But do not worry, they were not bad men. They were not SS or Gestapo, but they still had to fight. All our men had to fight. They decided to join the *Kriegsmarine*, the navy. They were in U-boats on the same crew. Their U-boat didn't come back from its patrol last year.'

Robbie realised that Nina and her father would probably never know what had happened to their young men. 'I'm sorry Nina,' was the only response he could come up with, so he took her hand in his and they sat in the churchyard with their memories for a while longer.

After a while, Nina added, 'I would have hated them to be SS. Those men were evil, you know. Even now we are not ashamed to point them out to your people when we find them. They killed so many Germans as well as other people; women and children, it did not matter.'

'I know, I met them when I landed,' Robbie told the young woman. 'They gave me a fairly warm welcome.'

'You are lucky they didn't shoot you,' Nina replied. 'They were ruthless. I am ashamed that we knew of the camps where they killed the Jews and so many others and we let them carry on…'

This time Robbie was unable to think of a reply so he stood up. Leaving the churchyard, Robbie realised that the chance to visit the area might not come again for some time. Having found the crash site and the graves of his friends, the final piece of his jigsaw would be the farm. Having seen the aircraft hit the ground, he knew it could not be more than two or three miles from the crash site. Pinpointing on the map, with Nina's help, the field they had just visited, Robbie was able to estimate a search area for the farm. There were not many roads amongst the fields and woods; they could cover much of that part of the countryside in a reasonably brief time.

Having only been at the farm in darkness, Robbie was not confident about finding it immediately and he considered calling the search off as the afternoon went on. However, he was correct in that scouring the area was an achievable task. The fourth farmyard they called at seemed to have its buildings in the right place and the lane continued beyond the yard towards some fields. It was along that lane, Robbie believed, that he had hobbled with his bruised ankle. They stopped briefly in the yard and Robbie knocked on the farmhouse door, though to no avail. After a few attempts at making his presence known he climbed back into the jeep and headed for the lane to the fields.

As the jeep rounded the corner, Robbie saw ahead of them two farmhands walking back towards the house. They carried a bag of tools and a coil of wire; mending fences, he thought ruefully. He stopped the jeep. As they approached, unfazed by the appearance on the farm of military personnel, Robbie realised that they looked horribly familiar. He looked at the floor of the jeep and said to Nina, 'I know these two chaps. Just make some excuse and we will leave. I'll tell you when we are on the road.'

The two men were totally focussed on Nina, who asked them a question. From their scowls, they had clearly drawn their own conclusions about what a British serviceman and a local woman might possibly be doing on a remote farm track. However, there was no longer any fight in the men and Robbie felt they posed no threat. After a brief exchange of what Robbie imagined might otherwise have been pleasantries, Nina told him, 'We have come the wrong way; we must go back to the road.' One of the farmhands grudgingly opened a field gate so that Robbie could reverse into the gateway and turn the jeep round. He waved in an unacknowledged salute to the men and they returned along the lane.

Once clear of the farm, Robbie stopped the jeep and told Nina, 'Those were Willi and Kurt. They were two of the men who captured me. Last time I saw them they had SS badges. I told you they were not very pleasant; the bruises took a while to go.'

'All SS men are to be reported.' Nina recited a mantra disseminated by the occupying power, as if obeying orders was still a feature of everyday life in Germany which, in a sense, it was. 'We must go back to the police station and tell the Americans.' She looked at the map. 'It is this farm, is it not?' Robbie confirmed the location, before resuming their journey.

This time the Master Sergeant showed genuine interest when Robbie told him about the SS men. 'So, you could identify them at the time as SS, and they mistreated you? That's a great start, buddy.' He went off to organise a posse, saying to Nina, 'It's kinda difficult for a German girl to have to sell out her countrymen but, heck, you're an interpreter so I could do with you along.'

The two Germans were in the yard when the jeep arrived at the farm, this time accompanied by a six-wheeler US Army truck which disgorged its cargo of well-armed GIs. Robbie confirmed the identity of the two SS men, earning a mouthful of phlegm from the ever-delightful Willi, who also snarled a passing comment at him. 'He says he wishes he had shot you while he had the chance,' translated Nina. 'I think perhaps that is not a helpful thing for him to say,' she added, smiling at the airman.

They returned together to the police station; on this occasion, it was the Germans inside the cells and Robbie outside. He watched quietly as Willi settled on to the same bench that Robbie had occupied on his first night. No sooner had he done so than he looked up with a start, staring at the far corner. His face had turned pale and he started shaking. He sat upright, cowering against the wall. Robbie twisted his head to see what had alarmed the German. The girl and boy stood in the cell, the girl pointing at Willi while the boy looked on. Then, as the SS man started shouting for the guards, they did their usual disappearing trick.

Robbie never saw the full transcripts of the interrogations of Willi and Kurt, but the Master Sergeant, having been praised by his superiors for his excellent detective work in rounding up the two men, was happy to share a summary with him.

'They were SS,' he told Robbie as they sat at the café. 'They were billeted at the farm whilst standing down from their normal duty, which was as guards at a labour camp halfway back towards Frankfurt. It wasn't one of the centres for extermination, or even a main concentration camp but, to put it mildly, they weren't the most amenable of hosts. That Willi guy went to pieces as soon as we started putting a bit of pressure on him. I've no sympathy for the guy, they are all bastards who are now just stealing oxygen from the rest of us. There was a third guy, apparently, but he was killed by a stray shell when we took this ground, you'll be pleased to know.

'He kept going on about seeing ghosts; a girl and a boy that were in the labour camp. He and his mates took it upon themselves to kill the kids as they couldn't work. They looked Jewish; that was enough for these animals.

'Anyway, they heard your aircraft low overhead then saw the flash when it hit the ground. One of them went outside in case you turned up which you did. They'd been promised a bonus if they handed you over in one piece to the Luftwaffe; it seems you guys were always seen as a source of intelligence so they couldn't just kill you. So, they gave you a working over to remind you who was boss.

'When they went back to the camp they found that a lone plane, probably yours, had dropped a goddamned bomb on the place. It hit the barracks. Massive bomb too, by all accounts....'

'Four thousand pounder,' said Robbie. 'I hope it took a few of the bastards out.'

'Sure did, buddy. The barracks were a distance outside the main part of the camp; they didn't like to be too close to the *Untermensch*, so the prisoners were unharmed. Some of them tried to rush the remaining guards to escape but they were gunned down. It gave them some brief hope though. The bastard said that, if they'd known that you'd bombed the barracks they would just have killed you anyway. He's lost the plot now; knows his days are numbered. That confession will get them both the noose.'

Robbie found he felt no remorse at the impending fate of the SS men; they had shown him scant mercy and their other victims none. He still felt sorrow for the innocent victims of the bombing raids but now realised that countless others had been saved by the defeat of the evil regime. He pondered the role of the children in the saga. He did not mention their appearance to the Master Sergeant as it would add nothing of evidential value and would only serve to diminish his credibility. Perhaps, he said to Nina when, eventually, he felt ready to tell her about the visitations, the children had not been able to break contact with their earthly past. Maybe their parents were still in the camp. The children must have latched on to him when he had inadvertently caused the deaths of so many of their tormenters, though by chance their own murderers had been spared. They had seen him through his own darkest days and led him, eventually, to the guilty men. He had brought them to justice and he was truly glad to do that for the girl and the boy who had suffered in just another war crime.

Duty Carried Out

The old man looked into the flames as he sipped his mug of tea. The wood-burning stove gave a sense of life and light that would otherwise have been absent from the house. Since his wife of over sixty years had died, the old man had lived alone, though he rarely found himself short of company.

As he drank his tea, Philip thought of his boys. He thought often, too, of Dorothy but she was at peace, a gift denied to his boys. He spent much time, these days, lost in the memories of those earlier times. A few, very few, short years but of such intensity that they represented, for the old man, the largest part of his life.

He could remember his boys with absolute clarity, their names, ranks and youthful looks. He knew with equal certainly what had become of each one, though at the time they had disappeared into the night. Sometimes singly, usually in some number, they had walked out of the locker room, climbed into their aircraft and vanished into thin air.

It had all seemed such a mystery at the time. Even though many aircraft were seen to be shot down, the explosion or flaming remains being visible for miles around, the bomber stream was tightly packed and it was rarely possible to say which aircraft and its crew had been incinerated or blown into oblivion. It was an anonymous death for most aircrew, at the time. Only much later could wreckage and identity tags be matched with the 'Aircraft Missing' lists in the squadron Operational Record Books. Even then it was arduous work for RAF identification officers and, later, the researchers and historians, to make sense of the records and ascertain exactly what mishap had befallen each airman.

But the old man knew their fates; he had done for some considerable time…

In the earlier days, back in 1944, he had commanded a bomber squadron. Twenty aircraft and enough airmen to crew them had been his responsibility, along with hundreds more ground staff to keep them all fit to fly, to fight and, mostly, to die. He had, by then, already earned his own spurs, having completed two tours totalling fifty operations. Somehow, despite his friends and fellow airmen dying by the plane load, he had survived, a statistical anomaly as the average life expectancy was twenty ops. He should, by rights, have died two and a half times over, but he had not. He did not know why or how he had been spared, nor was there any explanation. His boys didn't hold his amazing good fortune against him, he knew that.

He had eventually risen to the rank of Wing Commander. He had been awarded one DFC when he completed his first tour and a bar to the medal for bringing his critically-damaged Wellington home from Essen, one of the two engines shut down and the wings and fuselage perforated by shrapnel. He hadn't baled out because his navigator was seriously injured and the rest of his crew stayed with him. His navigator survived but never flew again. On his second tour he had visited Bremen, at night and without landing, and was returning to his base at Wrighton Common when his Stirling was crippled by a night fighter. The aircraft had sustained numerous hits, the cockpit being shredded by cannon shells which had miraculously left him alive though not entirely unscathed. He had nursed his Stirling home despite being half-blinded by shards of perspex from his shattered cockpit canopy through which the icy blast of the airstream did nothing to help his efforts. His co-pilot,

George, had not been so lucky, suffering fatal injuries, and Philip had to rely on the assistance of his remaining crew to hold the aircraft steady with the controls critically damaged. He had crash-landed at the emergency airfield at Manston. They gave him a DSO for that, but he would rather have had his co-pilot and closest friend back. He'd been through two years of training with George and had been best man at the chap's wedding only a few weeks previously. He kept in contact with George's family, feeling a highly personal bond with them. A couple of years after the war Philip married Dorothy, George's sister. He had every reason to be confident that his friend would have approved of that too.

George had died quickly, in his seat alongside his pilot. It was a 20mm cannon shell that ended his life, decapitating him mid-sentence as he commented on the tardiness of the Pathfinder Force in marking the target. He never saw it coming. The old man still saw George as he was immediately before his final trip, fresh-faced and barely needing to shave more than a couple of times a week, his dark brown hair slicked into the quiff popular at the time, rather than he had been after the attack.

Two operational tours, the second of which he had finished as Squadron Leader in charge of a Flight of ten bombers, had given him essential experience and enhanced his reputation for courage and calmness under fire and stress. He was posted to Group Headquarters for a few months, overseeing the introduction of the Avro Lancaster to the Group's squadrons. Despite the relative safety of his new role, in which he was most at risk of injury from misuse of the abundant staplers and paperclips, he very quickly became bored. He trudged along to interminable meetings, the apparent purpose of which seemed to be to agree with whichever officer held the highest rank, and wrote innumerable reports which he suspected would never be read, let alone heeded.

It was only when Philip managed to arrange trips to bomber stations that he found his spirit returning to life. For the time being, outside the close circle of camaraderie and shared danger, he noticed more than previously the atmosphere of tension and barely-contained fear pervading the crews with whom he discussed the imminent arrival of the new equipment. There was clear enthusiasm for the aircraft which was already the mainstay of many of the Command's squadrons, though this was tinged with the unspoken sense of pessimism by many of the aircrew of their chances that they would live to see its arrival.

His application to return to operational flying disappeared into Bomber Command's bureaucratic labyrinth with barely a backward glance. Weeks passed without acknowledgment or apparent action until, one morning, he was summoned to a meeting with the Senior Air Staff Officer for the Group. 'Keen to return to the fray, old man?' The SASO waved in the general indication of a seat on which Philip settled. 'Can't say I blame you. At least you know what you're letting yourself in for.' The senior man stroked his moustache with his index finger as he consulted a sheaf of papers on his desk. 'Well, if you're to go back into action, we might as well get something useful out of you. There's a new squadron to form, flying Lancs of course. You'll have to convert to the type yourself and then get the outfit up and running.'

The SASO slid the papers across the desk towards Philip, who leaned forward to pick them up. The Administrative Instruction gave sparse details; twenty Lancasters to be operational with a further four in immediate reserve. The squadron would be based at RAF Station Ridgefield in the nondescript countryside between East Anglia and the East Midlands. Philip had never heard of it.

He arrived at Ridgefield to find a scene of chaos. The airfield had recently been vacated by its previous tenants, a Pathfinder squadron, who evidently had so little faith in the RAF supply chain that they had stripped every building bare of fixtures and fittings. Scarcely a light bulb was to be found, let alone shelves or furniture. Fortunately, the supply of personnel had not failed the new unit. Philip found two key members of the squadron's staff already ensconced in the rather bare accommodation. They were the Adjutant, a Flight Lieutenant with a true flair for organisation, and a Warrant Officer (Discipline) who was exceptionally talented at shouting at the 'erks' and ensuring that they got on with their many and varied tasks without delay. As a result, the squadron offices, messes and sleeping accommodation were sorted out in a very short time.

583 Squadron, as the new outfit was designated, drew its flying staff from a mix of previously-screened staff who, like Philip, had been rested between tours of operations and who were now returning, willingly or less so, to front line duties, along with new crews, yet to be tested in combat and a smaller number who were transferred from other outfits mid-tour. Philip was wary of the latter, sensing that no commander worth his salt would willingly give up experienced crews unless they were more trouble to his own squadron than they were worth. The sprog crews were an inevitable result of the conveyor belt required to replace the constant losses of Bomber Command airmen; they could be trained and gain their own experience, if they lived long enough. It was on the first category, those officers and

senior NCOs with a tour or more under their belts, that he would place greatest reliance. They would be his leaders of men within the ranks.

Philip arranged for the few returning NCO pilots to be commissioned immediately. It made no sense to him for a Warrant Officer or Flight Sergeant with thirty or more ops behind him to have to defer to a Pilot Officer fresh from a Conversion Unit. Two returning officers, who already held the rank of Flight Lieutenant, were promoted to the acting rank of Squadron Leader. They would be his Flight Commanders.

The aeroplanes started to arrive shortly after. Each was towed into the maintenance hangar where it was fitted with the assorted ironmongery to bring it up to operational readiness. A few days later, each would emerge and take its place at its allotted dispersal, to be fussed over and tended by the ground crew. Then the aircrew would climb aboard, start the four Merlin engines and each Lancaster would come to life.

The day's work finished, Philip encouraged his pilots to gather in the Officers' Mess for a drink before dinner. He believed it was a useful opportunity to get to know his crews, albeit only those holding the King's commission. Most of his men were, however, Non-Commissioned Officers; Sergeants, Flight Sergeants and Warrant Officers. The RAF frowned on close relationships between officers and men, but Philip knew that all of them faced exactly the same risks and, to him, all were equally worthy. He made a point of visiting the various sections where the aircrew sharpened their skills whilst not flying. This allowed him to speak as a fellow practitioner to the air gunners, flight engineers, wireless operators, bomb aimers and navigators regardless of their standing in the hierarchy. He soon knew them by name though, of course; to the men and women he was always 'Sir'. It was a formal courtesy that was understood and accepted by all.

Philip urged his Flight Commanders, Alan and John, to compile training programmes that would sharpen the skills of their crews, most of whom had yet to encounter the enemy. To this end, he despatched them to other squadrons, especially those with the heaviest and the lightest losses. 'Compare and contrast their techniques, briefings, intelligence setups; anything they have in place for their own crews,' he briefed his two deputies. 'I want you to identify the worst practices as well as the best. The chaps need the best advice and training if we are to carry out our tasks whilst minimising the chop rate.'

When the first Lancaster was ready for flight he gave the honour of getting the squadron airborne to a young Australian Pilot Officer who had proved particularly hard working and enthusiastic since his arrival. Philip went along for the ride but made a point of not interfering with the lad as he put the aircraft through a series of tests. His presence on board was simply to demonstrate his faith in any of his crews to do their job safely and effectively.

Philip extended the same consideration and courtesy to his ground crews. Traditionally they owned their allotted Lancaster, in their own opinion, merely lending her to the various crews for their trips into the darkness. Ground crews tended to their machine as if she was a prize steed and were inevitably disconsolate on the all too frequent occasions when dawn broke over an achingly empty dispersal. Keeping an operational bomber in the air entailed many hours of care and attention, often in freezing or rain-soaked conditions. Whilst he did not go so far as to roll up his sleeves and rummage within the interior workings of the Merlin engines, Philip tried to drive around the dispersals during the daylight hours to pass on his gratitude and enquire after the well-being of the armourers and fitters as they toiled to get as many Lancasters into the air as possible.

It became apparent that his squadron was approaching the day when it would finally be able to join the war. Whilst those of his pilots with previous ops under their belt knew exactly what to expect in the skies over Germany, and how to increase the likelihood of returning unscathed, his new boys had no such prior knowledge. This put them at a serious disadvantage and Philip knew he had to help them get the necessary experience before letting them loose. He therefore arranged, via the adjutant, for two pilots to accompany crews of a neighbouring squadron on their next raid. All he needed was a couple of volunteers.

Pilot Officer Andre Lafarge RCAF and Sergeant Alf Hartfield could not have come from less similar backgrounds. Lafarge was of French-Canadian descent and had still been at school in Montreal when the war broke out. His family still retained an ingrained loyalty to the old country, and when the Wehrmacht strutted arrogantly past the Arc de Triomph the shame and humiliation became too much to hear. Lafarge volunteered for the RCAF as soon as he was of age, which in his case was 1942. He had enjoyed the experience of flight training, though it had required considerable effort as it appeared he was not a natural airman. He persisted, and made the grade. Nearly two years later, and now about to become operational, he looked forward to exacting his revenge on the Boche.

Alf Hartfield had been smitten with the idea of becoming a pilot since watching flying displays in his childhood but, as he was the son of a Nottingham miner, he concluded that this was destined to be an unrealised dream due to his background and limited circumstances. When war came, he joined the RAF as an engine fitter as it was the best alternative. Three years on, the attrition rate suffered by Bomber Command brought home to the higher echelons the reality of prolonged mechanised warfare. This was that they could no longer depend on a supply of 'the right sort of chaps' to meet the demand for crews. In fact, Bomber Command had relied on non-commissioned aircrew from the early days but the service had seemed strangely reluctant to release some of its most skilled tradesmen just to throw them to the Grim Reaper. Unlike Lafarge, the lowly former mechanic found the air to be his natural element.

Hartfield and Lafarge, in defiance of the traditional Services mantra 'Never volunteer for anything', stepped forward figuratively when their flight commander suggested that they might like an experiential flight, this one being on a proper operation. Philip spoke to them on the afternoon of their trip, and wished them well. For Philip, too, it was a novel experience as this time he was sending, rather than leading, his men to war.

The two novice warriors had then gathered their flying kit and cadged a lift in one of the Squadron's Bedford trucks to the neighbouring airfield at Little Bransford, four miles to the east. The bureaucratic process had worked well, their arrival being anticipated, and each was introduced to their host crew for the evening's entertainment. They accompanied their new friends to the briefing, to find that they would, in a few hours and assuming all went well, have the pleasure of visiting Dortmund.

Alf Hartfield found the experience eye-opening to say the least. He was impressed by the quiet professionalism of the crew as they went about the business of manoeuvring their Lancaster to the German city and rearranging its masonry before hot-footing it home again. His pilot reacted promptly to several firmly stated demands from the two gunners to corkscrew in order to avoid the predations of night fighters. Most awe-inspiring, and downright terrifying, was the intense flak over the target area. What struck Alf most was the complete absence of banter between take-off and landing. He resolved to impress this on his own crew.

For Andre, the flight was something of a let-down. There was the long wait for take-off, the seemingly-endless circling as they gained height, then a steady flight in impenetrable darkness. The isolation seemed complete, the crew unable even to see the other bombers they knew were around them, let alone the Luftwaffe Ju88 that latched on to them as they crossed the Dutch coast. Andre and his adoptive crew were never seen again. His greatest regret, once Andre realised that his time on Earth was over, was that he had not been able to strike so much as a single blow against the Boche who now, it seemed, could occupy his ancestral homeland with impunity.

News that Andre had failed to return was a matter of some sadness to Philip though, he recognised, it could not be one of regret. There was a war on and each had signed up to play his part. The difference now was that, albeit not deliberately, he had sent Andre to his death. Previously he had been responsible for taking his own crew on risky operations, having himself been given the requisite orders. Even as a Flight Commander he had been told, for the most part, which crews would run the gauntlet on a particular night. Now it was his decision every time who flew and who stayed on the ground. That was the loneliness of command in very real terms. The first time was the hardest, though Philip knew that it would never become easy for him.

The Canadian's place in history as the squadron's first casualty was left to the interest only of his family and subsequent historians. Philip knew he could not blame himself; it had been a matter of chance that Alf and Andre had been the pilots to go, and equally the loss of the aircraft in which they had been flying was the misfortune of war. He knew that Andre had understood the risks and that his anger was born out of frustration at his ultimate impotence as an instrument of vengeance. Philip could only sympathise.

It was only a couple of days after the loss of Andre that Philip was summoned to Bomber Command headquarters at Bentley Priory for what was termed a 'special conference'. Immediately before setting off for the meeting, the SASO had telephoned Philip to tell him that 583 Squadron was now operational, adding that the adverse weather would probably delayed the unit's baptism of fire for a couple more days. As he waited in an ante-room to be admitted to the main venue, Philip encountered colleagues from his earlier service in the Command, men who had, on the whole, been Flying Officers and Flight Lieutenants only a few months previously. Promotion was rapid for the operational pilots as their colleagues and seniors fell victim to The Chop.

The assembled multitude, once ensconced in the large conference room, was addressed by the AOC, Bomber Command, Air Chief Marshal Harris. The tactics employed against German cities had been honed through

1943 culminating in the obliteration of Hamburg. The long, dark nights and almost permanent cloud cover of a northern European winter would now allow those tactics to be employed against Harris's ultimate target, Berlin. A series of experienced and qualified leaders outlined the strategy and tactics that would now be brought to bear on the Nazi capital before Harris once again spoke to the men who he required to do his bidding. The forthcoming campaign would, the AOC warned his men, cost between four and five hundred aircraft but it would cost Germany the war. The airmen gathered before the AOC knew only too well that the hundreds of aircraft he expected to lose would contain their own crews and indeed, many of those now present. They were men who led from the front.

Philip was determined to face the same dangers as his men, though conceded that he simply could not do so on every effort. The demands on the time of squadron commanders were such that they could not be in two places at once and many evenings he would be forced to remain on the ground whilst his crews faced the ordeal by combat in the skies above hell. But he would join them when he could, and he was under no illusions that he was immortal; he still did not expect to survive the war.

On his return to Ridgefield, Philip gathered his inner council of the two flight commanders and other section leaders and briefed them on the forthcoming campaign. Their grim expressions, as they listened and offered their thoughts, reflected the realisation that some of them were probably not long for this world; they just did not know who would survive and who would not.

Within the week the teleprinter spewed out a length of paper informing the squadron administrators that festivities would commence with a maximum effort against Berlin. A clerk brought Philip the good news, who immediately convened a further gathering of his council. Twenty Lancasters should theoretically have been available with their crews and to offer this contribution would have been a feather in the squadron's cap. Unfortunately, three were unserviceable though he had two spare aircraft fresh from maintenance so was left one short. He would fly one of the stand-in Lancs with a crew recruited from airmen from the spare bods pool.

The Station Commander, a Group Captain whose own flying career dated back to the late Twenties, waited until the briefing room was full before going inside. He retained a sense of the dramatic and waited for the anticipation to grow as the crews filed in and took the seats lined across the Nissen hut. The wooden chairs were set out, symbolically, in rows of seven. He had once suggested that it would be useful if he could identify the assembled men by their trade and this had been, in true RAF style, interpreted as an edict. Now it was the order of things that the pilots sat immediately to the right of the gangway with flight engineer in the centre and bomb aimer on the outside of the trio. Across the gangway sat the navigator, then the wireless operator and the two gunners. The Groupie's ordered mind also believed that this format would mean that the crew members could compare notes with their fellows ahead and behind, and each was alongside someone of a similar trade. The crews themselves would have preferred to sit with whomsoever they saw fit, but they did what they were told.

Philip had taken his own seat at the front of the room facing his men. As the rows of seats filled, the hubbub increased. Nerves did not usually result in silence; indeed the chaps preferred to mask their own concerns and natural anxiety by chatting to all and sundry. Before him, the room morphed into a sea of faces above blue battledress. He ran his eyes over the squadron's personnel. This was the first time in which his charges would be let loose on the enemy en masse and he was aware of the rising tension. They did not yet know their target, though almost all would have spoken to the ground crew servicing their particular aeroplane and would know that the bomb load was a bit lighter than the Lancaster could usually manage, this being necessary to allow the maximum amount of petrol to be fed into the fuel tanks. There was only one conclusion to be drawn; the target was a distant one, meaning more time over enemy territory, flirting with death every mile of the way. Philip knew that the anxiety would turn to apprehension when their worst fears were confirmed.

As he looked at his men, he realised he was searching for a sign, an indication of who would return to the airfield unharmed and who would meet a fate which would inevitably be brutal and quite possibly fiery. This could easily include himself and his spare bods, now sitting at the back of the room. He shook the thought from his mind; this was a time to be professional. He could only get the best from his crews if they had faith in those who led them and to allow any intimations of mortality would undermine his own morale and that of those in front of him.

When all nineteen rows were occupied Philip saw a corporal open the door for the Station Commander so stood and called the room to attention. The Groupie made his grand entrance, striding to the front then turning smartly and announcing, 'Thank you, gentlemen. Please be seated. You may smoke.' The men sat down, reaching into their pockets for cigarettes and, in some cases, pipes and tobacco. The familiar blue haze slowly permeated the room complementing the battledress they all wore.

With a theatrical flourish, the Groupie pulled a cord to sweep open the curtains covering the board affixed to the end wall of the hut. A large map of Britain and Europe, marked with the symbols of the bombing war, was revealed, a red tape emerging from Ridgefield. The tape, a quarter of an inch wide, was visible from the back of the room though many of the aircrew wished it was not so. A groan emanated from those members who had flown operationally prior to joining 583. Even if they had not visited the city themselves, they knew its reputation as a 'chop' target.

The tape, having departed Ridgefield, made its way directly across East Anglia to Southwold from where it turned north east taking the bomber stream away from the Dutch coast. Somewhere near the Frisian Islands it swung thirty degrees or so right. The more eagle-eyed, particularly at the front of the room, noted that the tape carefully passed between areas around Wilhelmshaven and Cuxhaven marked in red, denoting concentrations of flak. The tape was equally concerned to pass through a narrow gap between the defences surrounding Bremen and Hamburg before taking a slight right and heading bravely into an intensively red area that was Berlin. Clearly not happy to be over the German capital for any longer than was strictly necessary, the tape all but doubled back on itself, heading away from hostilities with the utmost despatch. The stream would then head west-south-west steering clear of Brunswick before turning to take the surviving force well north of the Ruhr. The Groupie reinforced to the crews, who needed no telling, that they should try to avoid flying over this area as no good would come of such sightseeing. If all went well, he insinuated, they would also miss Amsterdam and Rotterdam as they reached the relative safety of the North Sea, and thence home to Ridgefield.

It all seemed straightforward, Philip thought, but there would be no red tape in the night sky to guide them through the hazards placed by the enemy to trap and kill the unwary or the simply unfortunate. He looked at the column of nineteen navigators, knowing that they would be concentrating on getting the route right and praying that each one was blessed with competence and luck. Their lives, and those of their mates, depended on it.

From his seat in the cramped confines of his Lancaster, F-Freddie, Philip would have had an unparalleled view of the sky around him, but for the all-encompassing blackness surrounding the cockpit. The aircraft, laden with four tons of high explosive, incendiary sticks and a still almost-full load of fuel, crawled heavenwards through the thick cloud with agonising lethargy. His initial concerns about icing were not fully realised, which gave him cause for gratitude to the Almighty into whose domain the bomber stream was now encroaching. The controls had been heavy for a while but they had climbed through the worst of the icing layer and Philip anticipated that they would, at some stage, emerge into clearer air. He always felt apprehensive inside cloud, knowing that at any moment they could be struck by another aircraft. The consequences would be brief but catastrophic and he preferred not to dwell on them. On the other hand, they were safe from night fighters and flak.

Philip glanced to his right where the flight engineer, Bob, perched on his dickey seat, scanning the various instruments that informed him how the Lanc was coping. With his helmet and oxygen mask in place, little of the man himself was actually visible. Only his eyes, peering at what he could make out of the dials, showed him to be a living human. Sensing his skipper's passing attention, he turned his head slightly and gave Philip a thumbs-up, to indicate that all was as well as could be expected under the circumstances.

After half an eternity, the canopy cleared as the Lancaster emerged from the cloud. The quarter moon had set and above them was only a myriad of stars. There was just enough light to distinguish the cloud layer and Philip elected to level off his aircraft slightly above it in the hope that his rear gunner might be able to see any enemy fighter that tried to sneak underneath them, whilst it was still close should he need to dive into it to avoid an attack from above. With his night vision fully developed he was also able to make out the shapes of a few of the other bombers in the stream.

A few minutes later the intercom sprang to life. 'Navigator to skipper, we should be approaching the first turning point in six minutes. If PFF are on time the first flares should be going down anytime now.'

'Thank you, navigator.' Philip's laconic reply masked the tightening feeling in his guts. The trip had been easy so far; over the North Sea all the way but the turn to starboard that was just coming up would take them over the enemy coast and life would be less peaceful. A few miles ahead, Philip saw green and yellow flares cascading from an unseen marker crew. The Pathfinder aircraft had eschewed the safety of the cloud layer in favour of height, ensuring that the markers would remain visible for as long as possible. Whilst some pilots would have been tempted to cut the corner and save a few miles and minutes, Philip was a stickler for following the plan. He had a time to be over the target and would aim for that, whatever happened. Coming home would be a different matter entirely.

The planned change of course occurred as specified and Philip's crew headed for Germany. 'Enemy coast in two minutes,' the navigator advised him a few minutes afterwards. To the south, Philip saw bright flashing lights joining the stars though more at his own altitude. These were orange and yellow rather than white, and far more malevolent in intent. Radar-directed flak sought out an unwary aircraft that had strayed from the stream, possibly because of taking too short a cut at the turning point. There was an explosion, red joining the orange and yellow in a fireball that lingered, then fell away, fading as it went into the cloud. It was a sight that he had seen far too often on his many earlier ops. Philip knew that a bomber and her crew had died.

He considered that the fallen crew was too far from him to be one of his own, as they would all have reached the first mustering point within a few short minutes of each other. But he couldn't be sure, and he tried deliberately to avoid thinking about the ghastliness the lads would have experienced in the last few moments of their existence. One at a time more fireballs appeared, most of them a distance away but occasionally one would erupt closer to F-Freddie. Philip knew that these were only the lost bombers that made themselves visible as they caught fire or exploded; added to their number were those that fell away unseen into the darkness, the pilot incapacitated, controls shot away or engines disabled. It was shaping up to be a bad night. With his own crew Philip could have been confident that they were on the ball but with this makeshift crowd he felt compelled to remind them: 'Pilot to all crew, keep your eyes peeled for fighters, for heaven's sake!'

Through the control column he could feel the subtle changes to the aircraft's trim as the gunners moved their turrets from side to side. He was comforted by the indication that they were heeding his command. Behind him he sensed the navigator stand up from his desk, position himself behind the pilot's seat and peer out to the port side of the Lanc whilst Bob did the same to starboard.

The attrition continued, as one crew after another found they had an appointment with their Maker. Philip stopped counting at fifteen as he found the rising toll to be something he would no longer prefer to contemplate. He could only pray that their own luck would hold. One operation at a time, each a step towards some respite, and there was no point in thinking beyond the here and now. Philip reminded himself how hard he had lobbied to return to this precise circus, and momentarily wondered why he had been so keen.

And then the slaughter eased, at least for the time being. There was neither rhyme nor reason to the timing of the fighter attacks. Sometimes they continued to the target and well into the return leg. On other occasions, it was as if their assailants had simply evaporated. But as Philip knew all too well, there was still the flak to come.

There was a glow ahead of him now, indistinct through the continuing layer of clouds; a patchy orange luminescence increasing in size as the Lancaster approached it at three miles a minute. Specks of green, red and white descended into it as the Pathfinders dropped their target indicators. Philip maintained his course resolutely towards these as the glow of the fires beneath became brighter. As they crossed the hellish carpet, Philip could make out the silhouettes of other bombers. If he could see them, so too could any prowling freelance night fighters.

He urged his crewmen to keep watching above their own aircraft as well as all around them. He didn't particularly care if he was telling them something they were already doing; it was a matter of better safe than sorry. At times like this he sorely missed his old crew who had, over the course of their thirty ops, built up a level of understanding and trust that meant no such commands were necessary.

The descending flares are countered by balls of light arcing upwards. Radar-directed flak meant that the absence of effective searchlights afforded them no particular sanctuary. The flashes of the exploding shells grew nearer as the Lancaster flew inexorably towards the aiming point.

'Three minutes to the target, Skipper.' This was from the Navigator who had, by necessity, returned to his post.

'Roger, Navigator, opening bomb doors.' Despite the lethally hazardous environment outside the aircraft, each crew man had his own task to perform, so only the gunners could be spared to maintain the vigil against the predatory Messerschmitts, Focke-Wulfs and Junkers hell-bent on killing them.

'Bomb aimer to Skipper, got that thanks. I can't make out any details on the ground so it looks like I'll have to bomb on the flares.' If the backers-up replenish them, which was by no means guaranteed, thought Philip, but he didn't pass on his thoughts to the man lying in the nose of the Lanc. Philip reached for the lever on his left-hand side. 'Bomb doors open,' he told the crew.

'Bomb doors open, Skipper,' confirmed the bomb aimer, who had the advantage of being able to check visually that this had happened.

The flak bursts were getting closer now as the time counted down to the target. Despite his fleeting skepticism about the marking, another cascade of flares, all green this time, rained down towards the fire bed. 'Bombing on the greens, Skipper,' the bomb aimer who, as Philip recalled, was named Eddie, added helpfully. Philip made a minute correction to their course so that he was heading directly for the centre of the grouping.

A fusillade of flak slightly ahead of them found its target, by luck or by judgement. A Lancaster at their own height erupted into a bright rolling mass of flame and smoke as everything it carried that possibly could explode did so with demonic malice. Philip did his best to avert his gaze, borne less out of the inevitable sense of horror that coursed through him as of the need to preserve his night vision. The task at hand demanded every vestige of concentration and professionalism. Sympathy for seven more men catapulted into oblivion would come later. Only one member of the crew broke discipline to utter, in a broad Australian accent, 'My bloody oath..' Philip allowed him that one; any admonishment was likely to fall on stony ground.

The blazing remnants of the unfortunate aircraft and its crew fell away leaving the run in to the target clear, as far as Philip could see. Their earlier prey dispatched, the flak crews now turned their attention on to F-Freddie. The shells seemed to make a slothful ascent at first, the orbs of light gradually turning at the last moment and racing towards the Lanc like comets of ill-omen. The night sky near the Lanc erupted into flashes, loud bangs and turbulence as the fuses determined that now was the right time for each shell to explode. As the aircraft bucked and swayed in the turbulence, the bomb aimer's detached voice continued to direct his skipper in towards the aiming point; "Right a touch Skipper... right a touch more...left, left a fraction..." Philip admired Eddie's coolness amongst the bedlam surrounding them, especially as he was, himself, feeling less than comfortable with the attention they were receiving. Some bursts were far too close for comfort, one having sprayed shrapnel which gave the canopy a glancing blow. Had it been travelling more directly towards them it would have shattered the canopy and, worse, have mutilated any or all of them but instead the perspex was just pitted and scarred.

'Steady, Skipper, the flares are dead ahead...ten seconds...' A particularly enthusiastic and well-aimed shot caused the Lanc to shudder and Philip wondered for a moment if they had been hit. The Lanc ploughed stoically onwards as Eddie kept up his patter: 'Nice line, skipper, keep it like that...bombs gone!' The Lancaster leapt athletically skywards, freed now of its four tons of bombs.

Thank the Good Lord for that, thought Philip. Now all they had to do was survive the next thirty seconds flying straight and level through the explosions and shards of red hot metal whilst they waited for the flash that would enable them to get the aiming point photo. That, and the perils of the trip back through enemy skies. The flak, whilst still exploding in the vicinity, seemed to be slightly further away than before. He hoped that flak crews did not pick up on their aiming error. He had no way of letting them know, and certainly not the slightest intention of doing so.

'Jeez, Skipper, you're the CO. Who's going to give you a bollocking if you don't take a bloody photo home?'

Philip considered imposing silence on the intercom but their future lives were in abeyance for the next half minute and he knew that their nerves were being stretched towards breaking point. He wanted to take the crew with him, not browbeat them. He remembered that the mid upper gunner, largely quiet in briefing and prior to their departure, had occasionally uttered the odd sentence, those being in an

Antipodean accent. Maybe he just came to life when he was living on the edge. 'All your Ocker mates if I insist on them risking their necks while trying to save your miserable skin by cutting corners. Now cut the chatter and keep your eyes peeled. Feel free to let me know if you spot any fighters, won't you?' he concluded.

'Good call, Skip,' the gunner signed off. Philip noted that no one else thought to disturb the atmosphere. They were probably praying for the chance to live a little longer.

'There's the flash, Skip,' Eddie informed him. Without waiting for a personal invitation, Philip banked the aircraft hard to starboard, pulling back slightly on the control column to tighten the turn.

'Steer two four zero, Skipper,' the navigator told him. Philip levelled out on to this heading and called the gunners to check above and behind the Lanc. On being told it was clear he pulled back on the stick, trading speed for height until the former fell away towards an uncomfortable level. He settled the aircraft at their new height and heading, allowing the airspeed to build up again and hoping that the such change in two dimensions would cause the flak crews enough of a delay to allow them to retreat out of range. It seemed to be successful as they were bothered no more.

The trip home was surprisingly uneventful and they landed at Ridgefield in the middle of a very cold, wet night. The crew, he was pleased to note, remained alert the whole way back. Despite the Aussie banter he considered that they had done their work well, whilst admittedly not having been tested by fighters. He told them as much in the lorry that took them from Freddie's dispersal to the debrief.

The old man took a sip from his tea, which was cooling now. For a unit's operational debut, things could have been worse, he reflected. It had not gone flawlessly, however, and the ORB noted against two crews their time of take-off then simply ‘Aircraft Missing’.

After their own debrief Philip had sent his crew to their billets, their work done for the night. His own task was far from over. He went up to the Watch Office where the Group Captain oversaw the WAAFs and a couple of male clerks who awaited the returning aircraft. Of the nineteen despatched from Ridgefield only one had the temerity, in the eyes of the Groupie, to cry off. Had he known of the Station Commander’s disdain, the pilot would have described the situation differently. A failed port outer engine, and its faltering inner neighbour, gave him no choice but to return. Philip’s was the sixth crew to return, and another two joined him in the interrogation room before he had finished. By the time he arrived in the Watch Office the airfield was still alive with the sound of engines, adding the growling and spitting of its own Merlins to the steady drone of those still airborne and heading for other landing grounds. The first thing he did on entering the busy room was to check the ops blackboard. Four aircraft were yet to return and it was getting late.

‘Anyone called up yet?’ he asked the Flight Lieutenant who was still nominally in charge of the show, despite the presence now of two senior officers.

‘Afraid not, sir. Another thirty minutes by my estimate...’ The officer’s voice tailored off; it was not necessary to explain in full that in half an hour all the outstanding Lancasters would have used their remaining fuel.

Time passed now with an agonising slowness until, with ten minutes to spare the telephone jangled. An orderly answered it, acknowledged the unheard message and announced to the room at large, K for King is down at Woodbridge. Shot up but the crew is in one piece.’

Within a minute the loudspeaker connected to the office wireless receiver announced, 'Nutmeg from D-Dog, D-Dog, request pancake.'

'D-Dog, D-Dog from Nutmeg, clear to pancake, no other aircraft in the circuit,' replied the WAAF whose task it was to welcome home the returning crews. After D-Dog landed, the wireless fell silent.

No further details are set down in the ORB, written immediately after the returning crews were debriefed, as the fate of the missing aircraft and crews was not known. The old man knew now the misfortune that had befallen the crews of Sgt. Tommy Peters in J-Jig and Flying Officer Sandy Heptonstall in B-Beer.

The former had fallen victim to a prowling night fighter, as was so often the case. An unseen foe had crept unseen under their wing and used the upward-pointing twin 20 millimetre Oerlikon cannon fitted to his Ju88 to despatch J-Jig and her hapless crew. Peters and his mates never saw it coming. Peters, having completed five earlier operations before moving to the fledgling unit, was haranguing his navigator who had been less than confident that they were on track. 'You've got to keep a much closer eye on those winds, old chap...' were the final words he uttered in his short-lived earthly existence. Before he could finish, all hell let loose inside the aircraft as the cannon shells ripped holes through the wafer thin aluminium skin of the Lancaster, did likewise to the flesh of the five crewmen in the nose of the aircraft and then exploded against denser parts of the airframe or exited through the upper surface of the fuselage. Peters never knew the fate of his two gunners, who had been spared the evisceration suffered by their mates up front only to die a lonely death, trapped inside the plummeting and spinning bomber by the insurmountable g-forces.

If Tommy Peters was surprised by his abrupt transition from life to death, the overriding emotion experienced by Sandy Heptonstall in his last moments was frustration bordering on intense annoyance. B-Beer had been hit by flak over the target. The shell bursts had impacted between the aircraft's two starboard engines, disabling both and causing a fire in the outer Merlin. Prompt and effective action by Heptonstall and his flight engineer in cutting off the fuel supply and extinguishing the fire meant that the situation had been potentially survivable. Unfortunately, Beer was a notorious hangar queen with a predilection for mechanical failure at the drop of a spanner and it came as no great surprise to the crew when the flight engineer announced, shortly after they had struggled back to the Dutch coast, that the port inner engine had coincidentally, and for no apparent reason, decided to produce only twenty percent of its normal power output. One good engine and only a paltry contribution from its neighbour, were not sufficient to sustain level flight and the range left to the Lancaster on that basis fell way short of the distance across the North Sea to safety. Heptonstall struggled manfully, ordering the crew to throw overboard anything that could be prised loose from the fuselage but it was to no avail. To add insult to injury there was no power available to the wireless for the wireless operator to send a distress message in their last moments of flight. The North Sea is a cold, wild and unwelcoming place at the best of times and a stormy night in the middle of winter could hardly be described as a suitable occasion to ditch a stricken aircraft. Having wrestled with his ailing plane for nearly four hours, Sandy Heptonstall was physically and mentally near exhaustion just at the time that he needed his wits and strength to be at peak performance. In the pitch, black night, he simply could not see the surface as he brought Beer down, and the Lancaster smashed into the concrete-like face of a thirty-foot wave at one hundred and fifty miles an hour, bringing instant oblivion to the crew. Heptonstall was, to put it mildly, irritated that his best efforts had come to nought and he was also a bit miffed that he had let his crew down. Their two years of tortuous training and interminable drills had stood them in good stead through their time at the Operational Training and then Heavy Conversion Units. Heptonstall himself had been fortunate in experiencing a second dickey trip with his HCU commander on a recent trip to Krefeld and this had been sufficient under the circumstances to qualify him to lead his own crew to Berlin. Never short on self-confidence, and having been a moderately successful captain of his school rugby team, he now felt he had only himself to blame as B-Beer took her crew to their watery grave.

Philip retired to his office for a couple of hours, too wired by adrenaline and the wakey-wakey pills to sleep immediately. Eventually he felt his eyes tiring and, previous experience telling him that no news was bad news, he went to bed.

The loss of two of his aircraft and, more poignantly, fourteen of his men, was the cross he had to bear. Colleagues reported missing was not a new experience but in his previous roles he had not borne the responsibility for every man on the squadron. He knew he had to man up and get used to the idea and the reality.

Berlin was the target of choice that winter of 1943/44. On sixteen dark, cold afternoons the curtain in the Briefing Room was drawn back to show the long ribbons stretching to the Reich capital by a variety of routes, usually to the north of Holland then almost to the Baltic before swinging south. On two occasions, only a few nights apart, the crews were aghast to see what was almost a straight line across Belgium and Germany, bisecting night fighter beacons and barely skirting areas of heavy flak, as if Bomber Command planners were trying to goad the Luftwaffe. The first time the squadron emerged unscathed, the defences having been caught out by this daring, direct, approach. The carefully-arranged diversion by a gaggle of obsolescent Stirlings and a cheeky raid on Munich by a few Mosquitoes confused the German controllers who guessed, wrongly, that Bomber Command would not be so blatant as to fly directly to their target and that the main force of Lancasters and Halifaxes was really a spoof. It was a good night for Bomber Harris and a bad one for the residents of Berlin.

The second time they were not so lucky and there were to be four ground crews left hanging around their tragically-unattended dispersals as the gloomy half-light crept unwillingly over Ridgefield the next morning. Flight Sergeant Peter Tunnicliffe, Warrant Officer Charlie Bennett and the experienced Flight Lieutenant Stephen Delacruz RCAF, veteran of thirty-five previous ops, all cursed the foolishness of the planners at HQ as they used the same route twice in a week. The Luftwaffe declined the opportunity to be fooled again and its defences, mostly the dreaded night-fighters, exacted a heavy toll in revenge with the three pilots perishing along with most of their crews. Of these twenty-one young men, only three survived. Two gunners were quickly captured on the ground whilst a cautious bomb aimer, who habitually wore his parachute whilst at his post in the nose of the aircraft, not only survived being blown clear when his Lancaster exploded but also hid out until Liberation in a farm house in the Belgian countryside. He would always be troubled by the notion that he had an easy war whilst his mates perished. The squadron's greatest hero that night was an easy-going Aussie, Sergeant Chris Creak RAAF, who managed to save his whole crew, holding their blazing Lancaster steady long enough for his six colleagues to bale out. He left it too late before joining them, having last been seen at the controls with his own clothing set on fire but still determined to save his crew. Creak died when his aircraft gave up the ghost and exploded. Philip nominated Creak for a Victoria Cross when his crew returned to England and told of his heroism, and Bomber Command staff, proud as ever of their crews supported his submission. The Awards Committee, by now inundated with heroic deeds attributed to those whom the politicians were by then insinuating to be the butchers of German women and children, sniffily wrote back '*...Sergeant Creak's actions were no more and no less than should be expected of the captain of an aircraft on bombing operations*' and grudgingly allowed that he be Mentioned in Despatches. Philip thereafter always referred to Sergeant Chris Creak RAAF as '583 Squadron's VC'.

Philip found he could not fly as often as on his earlier tours; indeed, as squadron commander he had no dedicated crew or aircraft and was usually expected to be attending to business whilst his officers and men went out to war. He did, however, spend every operation in the Watch Office, passing the time between the take-off of the first Lancaster and the time at which fuel would be exhausted in the last missing aircraft, pacing up and down and bothering the Watch crew for new information. All too often there was none. When all hope was lost he would ensure that the duty clerk dug out the relevant paperwork for the aircraft, arrange for telegrams to be sent to the next of kin of the airmen who had failed to return, and start typing the follow-up letters. As a flight commander, he had written these by hand, knowing every pilot individually and many of their crew members too. To his immense regret, as a squadron commander he found that, all too often, even the pilots were no more than a rank and a name. The increasing toll also precluded a personal handwritten eulogy to each family and now, for the most part, a clerk would bring him a pile of typed letters for his signature. At times, he felt he was letting them all down but could see no real alternative.

When he got the chance, though, Philip would choose an operation and put himself on the Battle Order for it, making a point of selecting particularly awkward targets. He would ask for volunteers from the 'spare bods' pool of unattached crewmen, for each of whom it was a step closer to the end of their tour. The downside was that a scratch crew had no knowledge of the strengths and weaknesses of their fellows; on the other hand, they had all responded readily to his request, which indicated their confidence in their own abilities and in his.

And so it was that in February Philip set out for Leipzig with his makeshift crew, all NCOs apart from the navigator who was a quietly-spoken flying officer from New Zealand. His flight engineer, an Irishman in his early thirties, was a Warrant Officer who seemed calm and unflappable, an air he managed to maintain even as the raid appeared to fall apart around them. To his shame, Philip was never able to recall the flight engineer's name. Flying infrequently, and that with strangers, had inevitably led Philip to address his crew members by their role. It was impersonal but avoided confusion. A concise but polite 'Thank you, Engineer' was the Irishman's reward as he updated Philip with the necessary stream of technical information the pilot required.

Leipzig was in a far-flung part of enemy territory meaning that it had survived relatively unscathed for nearly four and a half years of conflict. No doubt, Philip reflected, the planners at Bomber Command relied on the element of surprise, hoping that the enemy would anticipate yet another attack on Berlin, whereas that particular battle was now winding down in favour of an onslaught against the German aircraft industry. Leipzig was home to manufacturers of precision instruments and the RAF was now tasked with wrecking this industry with its habitual sledgehammer tactics. The enemy, once he realised that the target was deep within Eastern Germany, would have plenty of time to react.

The toll was heavy. In all his extensive experience of ops, Philip could not recall seeing so many of his fellows exploding or going down in flames. The carnage had started as the bomber stream approached the Dutch coast, a display of terrifying enthusiasm even by the Luftwaffe's normal standards. As the Lanc wound its tortuous way across the darkened turf of Occupied Europe, Philip could only hope that his scratch crew, however good as individuals, would be truly effective as a team. He wove the aircraft from side to side throughout the flight, banking to port and to starboard to allow the flight engineer to his right and the wireless operator standing behind him to peer down through the blisters in the Perspex canopy. Feeling air sick through the constant manoeuvring would be the least of the crew's worries if they failed to keep a good lookout.

Their luck held until the target area itself, then promptly deserted them. No sooner had the bomb aimer released their bundles of joy than all hell let loose around them. A sudden explosion rocked the aircraft. Even through Philip's flying helmet it was as loud as the crack of doom. It was accompanied by the sound of rending metal and shattering Perspex as shrapnel tore into the cockpit from the now invisible shell burst. Philip felt a sharp blow on the top of his head, as if he had been smacked by an unseen hand. Momentarily stunned he slumped forward against the control column, pushing the Lancaster into a dive. This almost certainly saved the Lanc as the next shell burst well above. Coming to his senses, Philip recovered the aircraft to level flight, noting that the controls were still responsive, though stiffer than he would have liked. The port outer engine was wrecked and missing its propeller. There were flames from the port inner engine so Philip took the necessary steps to shut off the fuel and douse the fire with the Gravener extinguisher. The flight engineer was slumped forward, half into the access to the bomb aimer's compartment. He seemed to be completely unresponsive.

He then called the crew individually over the intercom, receiving coherent replies only from the two gunners. Asking the mid upper to check, as quickly as he could, the condition of the two men who normally sat immediately behind the cockpit, he leaned forward and downward to see if there was any sign of life in the well now occupied by bomb aimer and flight engineer, but was encumbered by his parachute and obstructed by the controls, so gave up. The mid upper called up to give Philip the unwelcome news that both navigator and wireless operator were out of action and possibly beyond hope. 'They'll have to wait, we might get jumped by a fighter at any time,' Philip told him. The gunner returned to his turret to mount guard.

The bomb aimer's job was done for the night, and possibly forever if his lack of a reply was anything to go by. The flight engineer and wireless operator would have been useful, to say the least, but without the navigator, flying home from Leipzig would be problematic. But what option did they have?

Away from the target area the Lancaster was shrouded in a welcome inky darkness. It cloaked them from the naked eye though not, Philip knew, from the Airborne Interception radar in the prowling night fighters. It also hid the rest of the bomber stream from him. It would be a long, lonely, trip home. He had the route mapped out in his memory, having gone through it carefully before and during the briefing. In his mind's eye, he recalled the tapes heading from Leipzig towards the English coast. They would take him too far north if he missed the turning point, which was fifty minutes flying time from the target. That would do for now so he tried to keep the aircraft heading 315 degrees. He noted the time. His life, and that of his crew, depended on it.

Philip found he was having to work hard to keep the Lanc straight and level. She was trying to favour her port wing, which had lost its power with the death of the Merlins, so he had to correct for that whilst still weaving. If they flew straight and level they were unlikely to survive the gauntlet the Luftwaffe had thrown down. After an hour of the ordeal Philip was feeling the strain. He was also becoming light-headed but put that down to physical exertion mixed with the shock of the recent trauma.

'Fuel's getting a little low in the port main tank, Skipper, d'you think we might have a leak there?' George's voice was reassuring after the prolonged silence at the front of the aircraft.

'Possibly.' Make that highly likely, Philip thought after acknowledging the co-pilot's observation. 'Might be an idea to use what's left while it's still in the tank, no point in donating it to the Hun, unless it poisons his cabbages,' he suggested to George. He reached across to the flight engineer's panel and made the necessary adjustments. Philip knew he had lost some height but the Lanc had now settled for an uneasy truce in her battle against gravity. He was reassured by the knowledge that, having left five tons of bombs in Germany and burnt off half her fuel, the aircraft could survive on her two remaining Merlins. It was just as well; they were all she had.

There was little cloud above him, whilst beneath he could faintly make out a lower layer which formed a featureless carpet between sky and ground. It was very dark and, unable to see the ground, Philip was totally reliant on his instruments for orientation. He was still extremely concerned that an enemy fighter could creep up unseen. Their best hope of avoiding a surprise attack would be to fly through the lower cloud. Whilst he had his instruments there would be no real difference between that and pressing on through the darkness already surrounding him. It was a tactic that he had often espoused to his crews. He eased the stick forward and descended.

'Would you like me to check the chart to give you a course after the turning point, Skip?' George asked him. 'I can remember the course, I just need you to remind me to make the turn,' Philip responded. 'If we stay in the cloud, we will miss the markers they've promised us.' The plan called for flares to be dropped at the turning point but Philip knew from experience that he could not rely on this method and would ordinarily rely on his navigator as a backup.

The Lancaster descended easily enough and Philip levelled her out once he reached the cloud layer. The Met man had given the cloud base as two to three thousand feet with tops at about five thousand so he didn't have a lot of height to play with. At this low altitude, they were safer from the night fighters but would be easy prey for any alert flak units if the cloud broke; with two engines, the chances of climbing higher were negligible so all Philip could do was hope.

Around the cockpit the tops of the clouds were dimly visible and gave him a comforting impression of speed. He allowed the phosphorescent wisps to wash over the canopy; no one could now creep up underneath the aircraft though the gunners would still need to stay alert for attack from above or on their own level. It improved their odds slightly.

At this low altitude he no longer needed oxygen, so unclipped his mask; he could still use the mike if he had to, and it was good to breathe unencumbered by the rubber cup over his mouth and nose. He concentrated on flying straight and level, and on staying awake. The effect of the clouds now racing past was hypnotic, however, and Philip had to keep dragging himself out of a now-encroaching torpor.

'Flares above us and to starboard, Skipper. Must be the turning point!' George's voice broke through into his consciousness and Philip jumped into alertness. He realised that he had no recollection of the past half hour or so and cursed himself for his lack of attention. They were lucky his slackness had not been their downfall. He looked to his right and, through the flight engineer's side of the canopy saw a string of red stars hanging in the darkness. His rough and ready navigation had taken them west of the briefed track but not so far that they had missed the flares dropped by some of the marker crews that had survived the earlier slaughter. Philip eased the Lanc into a bank to port, away from the descending flares, and settled the aircraft on a heading slightly north of west. Recalling the briefing room map, he knew that this would take them across the Ijsselmeer and what he hoped was safely to the North Sea coast, near Amsterdam. With the wind from slightly to their starboard but at only 20 knots, he calculated that they would drift slowly to the south as they crossed the sea and should make their landfall in East Anglia, which gave them a comfortable margin of error.

'Skipper to crew, we should reach the coast in about an hour. Are you still with me?' It dawned on Philip that he hadn't spoken to his crew since leaving the target area; another uncharacteristic lapse for which he chided himself.

'Rear gunner here, Skipper, I'm still around. Nothing to report.'

'Likewise, from the mid upper, Skipper.'

There was then an awkward silence, so he called the remaining crew one at a time, though more in hope than expectation. His hope was not realized as no one else replied to his queries. 'Looks like it is just the three of us then. Keep your eyes peeled, chaps. I'm going to keep us on top of this stratus, it looks unbroken for now, but there are still plenty of fighter airfields.' The two gunners acknowledged this, even if it was glaringly obvious. Their discipline was holding firm, for which Philip was grateful. He stared ahead and to the sides but could see nothing significant now that the turning point was behind them.

'For Chrissakes, Skipper, wake up! There's flak ahead.' George's voice once more brought him back to full attention. He must have drifted off again. He was certainly feeling more light-headed than before so clipped his oxygen mask back in place; it made no discernible difference. Slightly off the port bow but much higher, he could see the flashes of anti-aircraft shells as the German defences took aim at the higher-flying bomber stream. He looked at the faintly-luminous dial of the clock on the instrument panel; it was nearly an hour since the turning point. The Lancaster had, by some means, stayed straight, level and on course while he had been asleep. Philip considered that was little short of miraculous. He also knew that if he had heard of any other member of his squadron falling asleep on duty, especially over enemy territory, they would have faced a serious charge.

Sensing George alongside him, and not wanting to alarm the gunners unduly, he unclipped his mask again and shouted above the noise of the engines and airstream; 'I'm not feeling brilliant, George, I seem to keep blacking out. You'll need to keep giving me a kick.'

'What do you think I've been doing, Skipper? I didn't want you to miss the turning point or the flak did I? I reckon that blow on the head you got over the target must have knocked you about a bit. Are you bleeding?'

Philip hadn't been aware, until he removed a glove and wiped his brow under the front of his helmet, that there was blood on his face. Wiping his hand on his flying suit, he traced the flow down his cheek until it curved with his throat and disappeared, probably soaked up by the fleece lining of his Irvin flying jacket. That would account for the light-headedness and was a cause for major concern. George's voice suggested, 'You losing it again is a bigger threat than any fighters right now. Why not get one of the gunners to stay with you and keep you awake?'

'Damn it, man, why can't you do it?' Philip snapped irritably.

'I'm not supposed to be here and, other than shout at you there's a limit to what I can do.' George, unperturbed by his pilot's stressful question, sounded more distant now. When Philip turned his head to address him directly, there was no sign of his old friend. He called to his mid upper gunner on the intercom and asked him to come up to the cockpit.

'I was hit over the target and I've been losing blood. I've been OK so far but am not feeling too good right now. I need you to keep me awake till we get across the sea. We're over the Dutch coast now so have got about another hour till we reach England. If I'm no better, we'll need to bale out as I can't guarantee anything in the way of a safe landing. Can you check the bomb aimer and engineer first and then the navigator and wireless operator? If there's any chance they are still with us we need to try to get the plane down but if they are dead we might as well know now.'

The gunner went forwarded but almost immediately re-emerged from the bomb aimer's compartment. 'There's not much left of either of them, Skipper, they must have taken the full force of the shell. The other two didn't look too clever when I checked them before either. I'll have another look though.' He returned soon afterwards, placed his hand on Philip's shoulder to gain his attention and slid the edge of his hand across his throat twice to indicate that the other two crewmen were also beyond help. Philip nodded and focused on the way ahead.

They escaped the attention of the coastal defences, who were clearly enjoying the opportunity to fire at the mass of bombers twenty thousand feet or so above the batteries and were happy to ignore a lone bomber that droned past the flak line only five thousand feet above but unseen. Philip was finding it increasingly hard to concentrate but the mid upper gunner, alive, alert and with a vested interest in remaining that way, stuck to his assigned task of shaking Philip back into focus whenever he seemed on the point of drifting off.

As they crossed the North Sea the cloud layer eventually started to break up; it had served them well, however, and Philip knew that it would certainly be useful to see the ground when it was time to land. The light increased as the sun rose behind them. Philip checked the fuel tanks and noted that they still had an acceptable supply of petrol which gave him one less thing to worry about. As the English coast became better-defined he saw that they were between Great Yarmouth and Cromer. He adjusted his course to the south so that they were heading inland rather than towards the watery expanse of The Wash. He knew there were numerous airfields in the vicinity, but that the Bomber Command stations would also be handling large numbers of returning aircraft, many in a similarly parlous state to his own. Not far inland, however, he recognized RAF Coltishall which was, as far as he was aware, a fighter station. He hoped that the local airfield staff would recognise a Lancaster when they saw one, and not confuse it with a Luftwaffe intruder, none of which had more than two engines. It had been known to happen and any number of returning four-engined heavy bombers had been shot down by trigger-happy anti-aircraft crews who could not, it appeared, count beyond two.

He flew a cautious circuit around Coltishall and, as a further precaution, told the mid upper gunner to fire a succession of red flares to signify their distress. He was relieved to see a green flare rising from the balcony of the watch office, which he took as permission to land. With the last vestiges of awareness, Philip ordered the gunners to take up their crash positions and flew a final approach which he would generally have considered to be just about satisfactory, had he witnessed it at the hands of a less-experienced pilot, and settled the Lancaster onto the runway. Then he blacked out.

Without Philip's input to the controls, the bomber drifted to one side of the runway and slipped onto the grass, slowing gradually. The plane was still decreasing in speed when the grass gave way to one of the cross-wind runways. The concrete surface sat a few inches proud of the surrounding grass, forming a sudden lip which the Lancaster hit with a massive jolt. This threw Philip forward sharply and caused him to crack his head on the instrument panel. Being unconscious already, it made little difference. He did, however, break a rib against the control column. The Lanc's speed was too low for the sudden movement forward of the stick to have any effect on its attitude and the plane slowed to a stop.

Philip came round in the station sick bay some hours later, though initially with no clear recollection of what had occurred in the hours before his unexpected arrival at Coltishall. The two gunners, unhurt despite the departure of their aircraft from the runway and the consequently uncomfortable end to their trip, had returned to Ridgefield where they were debriefed. News of the injuries to the squadron commander was better than the alternative as initially it was feared that he had been lost. The staff at Coltishall had the courtesy and consideration to put a telephone call through to their colleagues at Ridgefield to make them aware of the outcome. The mid upper gunner could give a detailed account of Philip's struggle to remain conscious and to bring their aircraft and remaining crew home. The two gunners were called to speak to the station commander, the only officer senior to Philip at Ridgefield. After the interview, the group captain promptly wrote Philip up for a DSO. Neither gunner mentioned the series of one-way conversations they had heard over the intercom between the skipper and an eighth crew member apparently called George.

Philip's injuries amounted to a hairline fracture of his skull, caused when he banged his head on the instrument panel, along with severe concussion, a long scalp wound and loss of blood, the result of the fly-by of a piece of shrapnel that would have decapitated him had it been slightly lower. He had also broken the afore-mentioned rib against the stick.

The squadron adjutant, having taken it upon himself a couple of weeks later to update Philip's logbook, noted that Leipzig was the nineteenth operation of Philip's third tour. He promptly contacted Group HQ with a request for a decision on whether Philip should be credited with completing his tour, and accordingly being screened from further ops. Agreement was quickly given by the Group's AoC who knew when one of his most experienced officers should be told to call it a day. The AOC broke the news himself when he visited Philip as he convalesced. 'You have more than done your bit, old boy,' he said as he sat in an adjacent armchair in the lounge of the hotel which served as a temporary respite for wounded officers. He puffed thoughtfully on his pipe, occasionally almost disappearing behind a curtain of blue-grey smoke. 'I know you were frustrated flying a desk at Group last time, but you've got a hell of a lot to offer. You can come back and join my staff or, if you prefer, I could send you to work for Butch at HQ. High Wycombe isn't everyone's cup of tea, but the old man isn't too bad as long as you don't fall out with him.'

'What would you have me doing at Group? I'm not big on counting paperclips, as you probably remember…' Philip didn't want to kick his heels for the rest of the war but he did secretly agree that it would be quite nice not to have someone trying to kill him each time he left the ground, not to mention being relieved of the burden he had carried with each crewman he had lost.

'I'm sure we can find you plenty to keep you occupied. You know as well as I do that things are likely to happen this year, and that is bound to affect the way we operate.' The AOC reinforced his personal smoke screen and continued, 'It's early March now, and the nights are getting shorter. My guess is that Butch will call the dogs off Berlin soon, and the attacks on the Hun's aircraft industry won't go on forever. We need to look at how we would operate more tactically, what equipment we've got or can bring in, have we got enough of the right aircraft and enough crews? It might not be as exciting as dropping your own bombs in person but you've got enough wool on your back to know that there is much more that you can contribute, and that's what I need from you.'

Philip knew an order when he received one, however politely put, and didn't fight it. His new boss would undoubtedly prefer to have staff he considered to have volunteered and resistance would almost certainly guarantee a mind-numbingly tedious posting elsewhere, certainly out of the Group and probably away from Bomber Command. A training outpost in Scotland or somewhere equally remote, he thought. He smiled and told the AOC he looked forward to joining his new colleagues.

As he returned, painfully slowly, to some measure of fitness, Philip often thought about the Leipzig trip and the assistance given to him by George. His friend had been a very real presence and without his calls at the turning point and just before the coastal flak belt, Philip was certain that he and the gunners would not have survived. No one had mentioned an eighth occupant of the Lancaster and Philip concluded, eventually and reluctantly, that he had imagined the incident. He decided that the loss of blood and the concussion probably hadn't helped him retain his grip on reality in any case.

His head injury took time to heal and, as with all such recuperations, there were leaps forward and steps back. The latter caused Philip to start to question his sanity at times. It was in the middle of the night, lying in his room, that he started to receive visitors from his squadron. They should not have been there, he knew. Not only was it outside visiting hours but every one of his visitors had been posted missing at some time in the preceding few months. It was rather alarming at first to wake up and find aircrew in his room, all fully and properly dressed in flying kit. The first to return was Andre, who shared with Philip his disappointment at not having the chance to contribute in any tangible way to freeing the land of his ancestors from the grip of the evil Nazis, as he would forever think of them. Philip was relieved that Andre did not hold him personally responsible for his one-way trip; he even showed some understanding for the Ju88 pilot who had found the Lancaster in which Andre was undertaking his second dickey flight. Andre considered that the fellow was doing what he felt was necessary, his duty even, and he probably had family living in a town or city that would inevitably have received a visit from the RAF at some point.

Andre had found the whole matter of being killed quite straightforward after the initial surprise. There was the confusion of the attack, during which the bomber had rather inconveniently exploded before the crew could get out. Sitting on the end of Philip's bed, Andre admitted that he was rather lost at the moment so had decided to stick around the few familiar landmarks in this country which had been the last contact he had with earth. He hadn't known where Philip was, hadn't consciously sought him out, but had been thinking of his squadron commander and was surprised to find himself renewing their acquaintance. 'Not as bloody surprised as I am,' Philip thought, but felt it would be churlish to say that to his spectral visitor so he kept the thought to himself. After an appropriate time, spent catching up on news of the events in the squadron since Andre's departure, the Canadian told Philip, 'Right Sir, with your permission I will leave you in peace. I hope you didn't mind me dropping in.'

'Any time you're passing,' Philip told him, hoping that the irony was not too pronounced. Andre had, however, disappeared. In retrospect, Philip was surprised at the ease with which he had accepted the return of the lost aviator. As a rational man, he could only conclude, once again, that he had imagined the visit. In the light of day he could explain it as a vivid dream, a result of the lingering head injury, but in the dark hours, lying in his bed, it was all too easy to believe that such visitations were real. This was certainly the case a couple of nights later when Andre returned, this time with Chris Creak. On this occasion, the ghostly pair were in no apparent hurry to leave and were quite happy to share their experiences with each other as well as with their erstwhile commander. Chris was particularly impressed that Philip had recommended him for what he described as 'a bloody top-notch gong', even though he had been told that the Awards Committee had knocked it back. This time Philip drifted off to sleep despite the airmen still wandering around his room talking shop.

During his meetings with the medical staff, particularly the doctors, Philip thought it wise to keep quiet about his night time social sessions with departed colleagues; to do otherwise would, he felt, have resulted in a one-way trip to the local asylum. The visits did not frighten him, contrary to what he would have expected had someone warned him to expect encounters with the recently and violently deceased.

He did, though, think matters were in danger of getting out of hand a few nights later, when he awoke to find Sandy Heptonstall and his entire crew loafing around, clearly at something of a loose end. Philip had by now concluded that the Afterlife was sadly lacking in entertainment for newly-arrived airmen. He asked Sandy if this was the case, but the officer just shrugged and said that there didn't seem to be much direction or organisation in the Hereafter, and indeed it was even worse than the RAF in that respect where at least bored personnel could usually be given some pointless task to keep them occupied. Philip suggested that, as their captain, it was always open to Sandy to find them something to get on with, even if it was a route march, or a trip to haunt somewhere more interesting than his room. 'We could try an escape and evasion exercise, I suppose,' was Sandy's considered response, 'Though how much fun that will be when we can be sure to get away without being caught, I don't know.' At that the crew, to a man, disappeared once more into the ether.

Philip was somewhat relieved when the doctors signed him fit for a return to duty, albeit in a staff rather than operational role. Much though he liked and respected his old colleagues he would prefer not to be haunted by what might easily amount to a full squadron of ghosts, not least because it would probably only be a matter of time before someone else cottoned on that he was talking to thin air and he would wind up being returned to hospital.

In keeping with his return to health, emotional as well as physical, his nocturnal visitors became less frequent as the weeks and months progressed, though they didn't stop completely. Some, such as Andre and George, came back relatively often, sometimes two or three times a month, whereas others appeared to him once and that was it. He realised that eventually he would probably know what had become of most of the men lost from his squadron, and he found he welcomed that. He had, after all, cared about their well-being and he was gratified to learn from the men themselves that this had been known at the time and since, and was appreciated.

Philip's war in the air, though, was over. He adapted with enthusiasm to his new role, which involved readying the squadrons in the group for what everyone recognised to be the forthcoming invasion. The penny had dropped that he could now contribute much more by making a decent fist of the necessary organisation than he could by simply delivering an additional five tons of high explosives to an already-pulverised railway marshalling yard. He even admitted to himself, with diminishing reluctance, that he was at ease with no longer putting his neck on the line every time he took off.

Weeks turned into months and the war ground its way relentlessly to its conclusion. VE Day found Philip still ensconced behind his Group HQ desk, wondering what to do with the eighteen-inch high pile of folders that he realised would now be of little interest to anyone. He did not have to ponder for long, as the SASO, by now a close colleague and confidante, was sent to call him into the AoC's office for an impromptu liquid debrief, which took its natural course as these occasions do. Later that night he woke up in his darkened room, still groggy from the day and evening-long drinking session. Perhaps inevitably, he was not alone. Quite a throng of his late crewmen were apparently there to share the good news. Their only regret, several told him, was that they no longer had access to alcohol to help him celebrate. They were, however, quite happy to talk and the consensus was that, if they had to die, there was some consolation in it having been in a noble cause.

***

The old man's tea was quite cool now. He had been lost in thought, he realised, for some time. The fire, too, was fading but he still felt some warmth.

His boys had never really gone away. There were periods, sometimes months at a time, when they had not been to see him. His marriage to Dorothy, once the war was over, had been something of a barrier to continued visitations. The lads never called by when there was anyone else around and the presence of Dorothy in the marital bed meant that he was alone far less frequently. Philip had never confided in anyone about his contact with the airmen; he still considered that he would be regarded, at best, as a crank and, at worst, as seriously unstable. For that reason, he kept it quiet. He found their continued contact a comfort but, somehow, could not bring himself to tell his wife of the occasional presence of her late brother. Deep down, he did not want to lose the link.

Out of the corner of his eye, Philip sensed movement. George had materialised in the room. They greeted each other, and Philip invited his old friend to sit by the fire as he had so often since Dorothy's own passing.

'She sends her love,' George told him, still standing. It had been of even greater comfort for Philip to know that brother and sister were reunited, although Dorothy had yet to return in spiritual form to him. George had previously tried to explain that, with her peaceful transition, she had no compulsion to keep directly in contact with her former realm, but that she would be there when his own time came. And then, 'Let's go outside, Philip,' said George with uncharacteristic determination.

This apparent instruction surprised the old man, as his conversations with George usually amounted to reminiscences and small talk. He nodded and reached for his walking stick which was propped against the arm of his chair. Rising a trifle unsteadily to his feet, he shuffled across the kitchen, with the still-young George offering an arm for stability. Philip opened the kitchen door and stepped out into the wind and rain which he had hitherto failed to notice in the cosy security of the house. He didn't feel the cold, though, despite the lack of his coat. There were figures in the yard as he emerged from the shelter, many of them, and he knew them all. His lads had returned en masse in what he felt must have been the ultimate reunion. They walked forward and greeted him as they always had, with respect, genuine warmth but this time, it felt like a welcome home.

'Come with us, Philip.' George's voice was still compelling. The old man had no intention whatsoever of arguing, and went to resume command of his squadron.

Chop Girl

This is a true story. I have written it down as soon as possible after the strange events that occurred because otherwise it is sure to be lost. No matter how extraordinary it might seem, and whatever the effect on the sole witness, namely me, the details will fade from my mind in time. I am already beginning to wonder if I imagined what I saw, heard and sensed as there was no sensible explanation. It is also all too possible that I will not survive to tell the tale.

I am a rational man, a technician with access to the latest in scientific equipment and knowledge. My fellows and I use these to wage war, to bring death and destruction to those who use such things, or even worse, against us, whenever they get the chance. Death and destruction are very close too. I know that the chances are exceedingly slim of my surviving the cataclysmic events around me; why on Earth I have stuck my neck on the line by tempting fate so ostentatiously defies sense. Call it the arrogance of youth, but I have defied the curse so far, though it has claimed so many others.

The first time I noticed her was when she handed me a parachute. Nothing unusual in that; she was doing her job and I was about to do mine. I'm a Wireless Operator in a Wellington bomber. I need the parachute in case my career goes off in a different direction to the way I would like. Her job was to hand out parachutes and put up with the witty and oft-repeated question from wags as to the complaints procedure if it didn't work.

I wouldn't say that our eyes even met that first time, let alone that we felt a mutual attraction of any sort. She barely looked up as she heaved the bulky package onto the desk and indicated that I should initial the form that had just been similarly signed by the man before me. It was nothing new; I had taken a parachute from stores countless times in training and then each operation of this tour. She wasn't even dressed to impress. Like all her fellow WAAFs she was drearily attired in ill-fitting blue serge battledress. No badges of rank adorned her uniform; she was a lifter and a shifter, a dispenser of paperwork, a basic level functionary. The sort of person who filled air stations in their thousands and without whom the RAF could not possibly function. God bless her and all like her. She, in particular, could do with such Divine indulgence.

I didn't know, then, what she was called, that she claimed to be twenty-one, nor did I know where she called home. Had I known the last detail, I would have run a mile. Her hair was jet black but its straightness and length were impossible to gauge whilst it was held rigidly in place under her cap by numerous pins. Her eyes, I could tell from the briefest of glances as I passed by, were deep brown.

I took my pack and went to bomb something in Cologne.

Three or four nights later we were stood down from ops; it was someone else's turn to take their chance. My mates and I went to the Sergeants' Mess for an all-ranks dance. I could go for a drink there at any time I was stood down, the privilege of holding that rank. On this occasion, the 'erks', as we called the lesser mortals, were also allowed in for a brief period of time.

We were nearly two thirds of the way through our tour, in theory at least. Most crews were stood down from ops after thirty successful trips, if they lived that long, which most didn't. My mates and I had, so far, endured and survived eighteen ops. All of them were hell, even without the momentary terror of being bracketed by flak or the mind-paralysing experience of seeing another bomber sent down in flames by a prowling night fighter. The cold seeped through our flying clothing and chilled us to the bone, we were fatigued by the noise of the engines through the thin skin of the aircraft and the vibration that shook our teeth. This was no place for anyone with a whit of common sense or the vaguest tendency towards self-preservation. More worrying, if we dared to even think about it, was the average loss rate of five percent, which someone on the squadron had quietly calculated and word got around. That meant that we could expect one crew in twenty to be lost each time we set out on an op. Put another way, on average you were shot down after twenty operational flights. My personal cup of joy runneth over at that thought. So, a night off was very welcome, a few drinks were bliss and the opportunity to meet some girls was heaven-sent.

She was sitting by herself, nursing half a pint of beer. I had to look twice before I realised she was the same girl from the parachute store. She wore the same shapeless and unflattering uniform but her hair was free of its grips. Unfettered, it descended in waves to just below shoulder length. This suited her much better than in its more formal style. The girl was undeniably attractive. And alone; a situation that was unlikely to remain that way for long.

I nudged Smithy, our rear gunner. 'Target for tonight, old son, if one of us plays our cards right, what do you reckon?'

'Undefended at the moment, I reckon,' he considered. 'Must be new, Jim; I don't remember seeing her around the base before though.'

'She was in the Parachute Section on the Cologne op the other night, I don't know if you spotted her then,' I told him.

Smithy finished the remains of his pint. 'No, doesn't ring a bell. I usually wait till I can get mine dished out by Judy.' Judy was the latest object of Smithy's affections; he was no doubt anticipating her attendance at tonight's dance. If all else failed I was sure he had a back-up plan to get together for some quality passion time with her.

Smithy was single and unattached in the outside world; most of us on the crew were the same, except for Ron Pierce, our navigator, who was engaged to a woman back home in Oz, or so he told us. Must have been difficult, that, half the world away and with every chance that he wouldn't make it back. Still, it would prevent her becoming a widow, Smithy had once told him with startling lack of sensitivity. Ron acknowledged, in his laid-back Ocker way, that was a fair point and would save a lot of grief. Of course, Smithy couldn't leave it at that and asked Ron if he worried about her meeting another bloke while he was away. 'Not worth thinking about that, sport, as there would be nothing I could do about it,' Ron assured him. 'I won't have to worry about her teaching you a thing or two you're unlikely to learn by yourself.' Ron could take it, as well as dish it out. We all could, it went with the teamwork.

It was my shout, so I went to get a couple of pints. On my return, delayed by the inevitable queue at the congested bar area, Smithy pointed over to the girl. 'Too late, you've missed your chance.' A Sergeant air gunner I vaguely recognised was sitting with her and engaging her in conversation. I placed him as the rear gunner in the same crew as Len Carruthers, a Wireless Operator I had spoken with several times since their arrival on the squadron about four ops previously. The sharpshooter was probably regaling her with yet another of those 'There I was, guns out of ammo so I chucked my thermos flask out of the turret at the Hun …' yarns so often issued by some of our tail-end charlies. To be fair, the girl looked absolutely transfixed by the chap's detailed overview of air operations, or whatever else they were talking about. I could sense where that would probably lead, if he played his cards right. It was, I decided, not my turn to get lucky with that young lady, so I spent the evening getting happily drunk with my mates.

A couple of nights later she handed me my parachute once more so I gave her my best smile. She smiled back, but then spotted her air gunner friend a few places behind me in the queue and that was that. Off we all went to Essen, which was bloody horrible as usual. Len's crew, along with two others from our squadron, didn't come back from that one. It had been a short-lived romance for the parachute WAAF and her gunner. I didn't know Len well enough to feel any great emotion. It had happened before and I am sure it will happen many times again.

We did three nights in a row; my logbook tells me that after another trip to Essen we then went to Bremen, but I wouldn't really know as it was dark and I spent most of the time sitting in my cubicle listening to the wireless set. We tried to wreck all of them on behalf of the British Empire; I don't know if we succeeded but it kept us busy. Someone else gave me my parachute each time, though I saw her in the line of WAAFs handing the packs out and taking them back in on our return, those of us who came back.

We had a few nights off during the 'moon period', when even the planners at Bomber Command HQ realised that we would be sitting ducks in the moonlight. I went into Lincoln a couple of times with Smithy and the lads, and got drunk on each occasion. It's what we did, and there was no reason to do otherwise; we don't exactly spend too much time thinking about the future.

Arriving back on the station, I signed the leave diary at the guardroom to show that I hadn't scarpered and then sauntered back to my Nissen hut. My route took me past the station cinema, which had just finished the matinee performance of some lightweight film. I saw the parachute WAAF emerge with another airman, this time a navigator but still a sergeant. There was a degree of inevitability to his rank. All aircrew were at least of the rank of sergeant and, as a WAAF 'Other Rank', she could hardly be seen fraternising with an officer. Decorum meant that they could hardly walk around the station arm in arm, but they certainly looked like they had recently enjoyed each other's company in the fetid darkness of a crowded, and very cramped, cinema. I didn't recognise the navigator.

There was a war on and it wasn't long before we were despatched once more to annoy Hitler by knocking all his subjects' houses down. Bremen beckoned, again, though this time our usual aircraft, F for Freddie, was not available. Whilst we were away another crew had brought her back from Frankfurt full of holes and needing a new engine so she was parked forlornly in the maintenance area till someone got a chance to fix her. We were given a different plane, T for Tommy, to tide us over until Freddie was fixed. T for Tommy was at a completely different dispersal which meant a change to our normal routine. We always hate a change to what we are used to. We have become creatures of habit and the sequence of events leading to our departure on ops has become a ritual. It gives us less to think, and therefore worry, about. Rituals breed superstition though, and we always hate change. Tonight, this meant a ride to the dispersal in a different lorry, with another crew sharing the lift.

I noticed, as the second crew clambered aboard, that their navigator was the sergeant I had seen emerge from the cinema with the parachute WAAF. I didn't make a big issue about it; petty jealousy was a trivial concern when our very lives were on the line. Good luck to him, I thought. I wondered if she had mentioned her previous ill-fated romance with Len's gunner. Probably not, and maybe his amorous attention had helped her cope with her all-too-recent loss.

The other crew was deposited at the dispersal immediately before ours, their aircraft being R for Robert. Their pilot, a Canadian Flying Officer left us with a cheery 'Go get 'em, guys!' as he lowered himself gingerly down from the tailgate, encumbered in his bulky kit. A minute or so later it was our turn to leave the lorry and visit Bremen, which was quite vile.

We returned in the small hours, cold, fatigued with our nerves taut after the trip through the dangerous darkness. We had staggered home on one engine after a flak burst that was too close for comfort, resulting in damage to the port wing and the motor thereon. We were, therefore, late landing and had been a cause for some concern amongst those who awaited us. There was no sign, though, of R for Robert or her crew. They are still unaccounted for as I write this.

The parachute WAAF kept a low profile for a couple of weeks after that, probably reflecting on the loss of two boyfriends in such a short space of time. Over a pint I mentioned to Smithy that I hadn't seen her for a while.

'Count yourself lucky that you were spared her attentions, Jim,' he told me, staring into his pint.

'How do you mean?' I asked.

'She might be a Chop Girl.'

'A what?'

'A Chop Girl. Every squadron has them. They get a boyfriend from amongst our elite number and he then goes for a Burton. They move on and, guess what? The same thing happens to the next one. And the next, unless someone notices what's going on.' Smithy took a mouthful of beer, swallowed and continued, 'After that no one will touch them with a bargepole. They get the cold shoulder off our lot. Would you go out with a lass who was jinxed? I bloody wouldn't mate.'

'Why should she be jinxed?'

'We've seen her with two chaps since you first started going on about her. They went missing within days, and their mates with them. Starts to look a bit odd, that's all I'm saying.'

I thought about that notion for a while. It wasn't something that had been brought up before. 'It's nonsense, though, when you think about it. Look at the chop rate on ops at the moment. When was the last time a crew got through its thirty? If she goes out with any of us, it's odds on that we won't come back one night. What about your Judy, does she ever talk about other blokes?'

'I've never asked, it's not the done thing, and she's never said. No one else has ever warned me off either,' Smithy stared back into his tankard again, as if it was a crystal ball. With his present line of conversation, I don't imagine he saw a bright and lengthy future. Before I could change the subject, he went on, 'On my gunnery course, one of the instructors started talking about a Chop Girl on his station during his first tour. Three chaps in a row picked her up at a dance, and all three were posted missing within a few days of making her acquaintance. After that no one would go near her. She worked in the Sergeants' Mess, a cook. It got to the point where the lads wouldn't even let her dish out their food, in case it was somehow tainted. The Adjutant got to hear about it and she disappeared, posted somewhere else apparently. We all thought he was winding us up about her but he swore blind it was true.'

Poor bloody lass, I thought. Loses a string of boyfriends which would be bad enough and then gets tainted as some kind of Jonah. No wonder Judy never mentioned anyone else, if that was likely to be the outcome.

'Keep an eye on her, then. Let's see what happens to the next chap she takes a fancy to,' I suggested.

'Yeah, well I wouldn't get any ideas if I were you, Jim. The odds are stacked against us as it is. You might be willing to take a chance but what about the rest of us? We're all in this bloody situation together, for better or for worse. Please don't forget that. I'm watching your back from the rear bloody turret, freezing my whatsits off while you sit up front listening to the wireless. Don't make it any worse than it already is, mate. Let's change the subject anyway, it's pointless worrying about it.'

I thought that abrupt change of tack was a deliberate attempt by Smithy to cheer himself up and I for one wasn't going to persuade him otherwise so I bought us both a pint.

The HQ planning wallahs obviously had something personal against Bremen as we went back there three times in the next week. The place didn't improve as we returned each time, its residents as hell-bent as ever on making us feel unwelcome. I think all of us on the crew were getting to the end of our tether but none of us wanted to show it. Someone might notice, and we would pick up a reputation for being windy. As soon as that happens you might as well pack up and go home. We'd seen it happen to other crews all too often, so we tried to pretend we were all fine. But our nerves were becoming stretched, and there was clearly tension within the crew. We were totally professional in the air because we all knew that to be anything else would be tantamount to suicide. But on the ground, Ron kept himself to himself and we hardly saw anything of our pilots, though this was partly because they were officers so didn't mix with the riff-raff on the ground. Occasionally our bomb-aimer, Keith Pearson, would join us. He and I tended to work more closely together as he doubled up as second wireless operator, in case I got injured or forgot my Morse code or something. Keith was had been brought up in a religious family. He didn't ram his faith down our throats, which was just as well as mine had become sorely tested, and I suppose it's handy having someone in the crew who has a direct line to the Almighty, just in case. Anyway, the upshot was that our boozy jaunts on the ground became less frequent and more restrained as we gathered in what was becoming a regular gloomy silence. We must have looked a happy bunch by then. Eighteen ops down, and another twelve to get through before a respite. It all seemed a long way away and far from certain that we would get there.

It didn't help when Smithy, Keith and I went to another dance at the Sergeants' Mess, for want of any other entertainment on another night off. Not surprisingly, the Waafery had contributed its finest females, and I noted that she was amongst them. It wasn't long before she had male company, though, as Smithy was quick to point out to me. 'I've got ten bob says that bloke won't come back from his next op,' he told me as we viewed the pair from a safe distance.

'You'll need to find out who he is, otherwise we'll never know,' I pointed out. Smithy rested his pint on the bar and made his way over to where they were standing. I saw my crew mate have a brief chat before giving the other fellow a thumbs-up and returning to our small group.

'Says his name is Lou Peterson, he's a Canadian bomb-aimer, just arrived here last week,' Smithy informed us.

'What, did you just go up and say, 'Who are you then mate, because me and my mates don't think you're long for this world?'' Keith wanted to know.

'Subtler than that, Keith, old son...I asked him if he was Sam Smith, a bloke our pilots had told us about. When he said no he wasn't, I said 'Are you sure?', like I was some kind of idiot, and he said yeah, he was reasonably certain because his ID card told him he was Lou Peterson, and he had no reason to think it was lying.'

'Pure bloody genius,' conceded Keith with more than a hint of irony and we shared a laugh. For a brief time, our old sense of comradeship made a comeback, so that was a positive.

We weren't laughing a couple of nights later when we returned from Duisburg, a hostile place, and found out that Peterson and his crew had failed to make it back. 'The Chop Girl strikes again,' muttered Smithy darkly when we heard the news, 'That's ten bob you owe me, Jim.'

I told Smithy I would remember him in my will which, in all honesty, was not the subtlest way of putting it. However, ten bob was ten bob, more than a day's pay for Sergeants, even in aircrew roles.

It did make you think, though. Three new boyfriends, none of whom were now around to enjoy her company any longer. They appeared to have taken their crew mates with them too. No one has any way of knowing where they are or even if they are still alive. We can only hope that they have made it to the ground in one piece and, perhaps, managed to keep out of the evil clutches of the Nazi hordes.

One day we will find out, perhaps. But the fact remains that the last three blokes we saw with her have gone missing. It didn't bode well for her reputation.

What to do, though? We were all on the same side, WAAFs and airmen, and the poor lass was probably grieving the loss of those men to whom she had drawn close. Who were we to make her life even more miserable, I pointed out to Smithy. He, however, took a more ruthless line. 'We can't let anyone else get cursed, whether she means it or not,' he told me. 'Far better that we try to get her away from here before she can do any more damage.'

'Well bloody good luck with that one,' I retorted. 'Precisely how are we going to achieve that? Do we go up to her and ask if she would be so kind as to take her horrible witchcraft somewhere else? Or maybe go and find the Queen Bee WAAF and tell her that one of her girls is doing Hitler's work for him and contributing to the butcher's bill? It's you she'll wind up getting rid of, on an LMF charge.'

'I dunno, Jim, but somebody needs to sort her out. Otherwise we'll have to put the word around. The facts do speak for themselves, you have to admit.'

'Let me think about it. Some of us will get it on any op, the way things are going. We'll just have to make sure it's not us.'

It was back to Essen next time out, then Düsseldorf, both which were less than a pleasant experience but, remarkably, we lost no crews on either night. But, then again, there had been no sign of the Chop Girl either with or without company. She wasn't even doling out or collecting in the parachutes when we flew. Perhaps, I thought, she had taken the hint or maybe she'd gone on leave, which would give our chaps a welcome respite. For our crew, this was very significant indeed, as our next op should be our thirtieth, and last.

Perhaps inevitably, the moon period intervened and we were stood down from ops for six days. We were even offered a leave pass, which resulted in a ferocious discussion amongst ourselves as we gathered in the White Knight, a local pub near the station, for an impromptu and rare evening out as a whole crew. Two schools of thought clashed, with three proponents each. One suggestion, favoured by Ron, Keith and Smithy was that we should grab the leave while it was on offer; we never knew what the future held so ought to make the most of it. The throttle jockey and I preferred to take our chance with whatever fate had to throw at us in the next week or so and finish our tour. We would then have a couple of weeks' leave before being posted elsewhere for the rest cure that entailed a training post somewhere.

Our skipper won the day, so we stayed on the base. For the first three days, there was nothing happening so we were allowed out each evening for a few beers, an opportunity we accepted with alacrity. The first two of these saw us bonding again as a crew in the White Knight. On the third the other lads, apart from Smithy, decided to go into town to see a film. Smithy, however, had arranged to meet up with Judy when she finished whatever bit of Waafing she was compelled to do. I didn't fancy the films on offer so went back again to the White Knight, where we were becoming regulars.

The start to the evening was quite convivial as Smithy's mood had revived considerably; he and Judy seemed to have a sense of optimism which, though I feared it might prove premature, seemed to cheer us all up. We had three or four pints, which was about par for the course these days.

Whether or not the beer was watered down to help the war effort, we seemed to be able to handle it in greater quantities than before we joined up. Eventually Judy turned up and I no longer had Smithy's undivided attention. I bade them a good evening as they wandered off to another watering hole.

I was in no rush to finish my drink so stood by the bar, engaging in conversation with a few of the locals, mostly middle-aged farm workers whose contribution to the greater good was to keep us fed. About quarter of an hour after the two young lovers had left me to my own devices I noticed, with a start, the Chop Girl. She was sitting in the corner though I hadn't seen her there earlier and certainly hadn't noticed her come into the pub. Thinking about it logically, I surmised that she had probably been screened from view by some of those standing closer to the bar. She had half a pint of ale and seemed to be at ease with the world. Significantly, she appeared to be unaccompanied. She looked up and noticing me watching her, returned my gaze. She gave me the sweetest imaginable smile, her face lighting up as if she recognised me as a long-lost friend. It was an entrancing look that banished all my initial trepidation. Her eyes seemed to reach across the bar and draw me in. I felt a compulsion to walk over to her.

'It must be nice to have a night off, Sergeant,' she offered, her eyes still engaging my own. She took my breath away and my misgivings about speaking to her were allayed. I could only return her smile.

'It's always nice to spend a night on the ground. I hope you're not about to hand me a parachute, though.' Cheesy in the extreme but then I never have been an accomplished sweet-talker. I introduced myself; there was no point in telling her what I did for a living. We were in battledress and my half-wing Signaller brevet marked me out as a Wireless Operator. She spent her every waking moment surrounded by airmen so that was not exactly an enticing topic of conversation. I closed my mind, for the time being, to her non-waking moments. She told me, in her turn, that her name was Eve Chandler, and invited me to sit down.

I was very wary about where this was leading and so must have seemed very nervous. Eve, to her credit, was gentle with me. Perhaps she put it down to a lack of familiarity with the female sex; she certainly took my rather uncertain demeanour in her stride and quickly put me at my ease.

She was, in all honesty, a lovely companion for a drink in a country pub. Without being garrulous Eve was an easy girl to talk to. She had, so she said, been on the station for about a year having joined up against the advice of her parents. They still lived a couple of hundred miles from where we were stationed so she did not, she said, get home often now and didn't know whether they had forgiven her for going against their better judgement. She didn't mention her earlier, ill-fated, friendships and I didn't see fit to ask. Why, I thought, spoil a very pleasant and totally innocent evening?

There was something special about this woman, a chemistry that I would have found very difficult to resist had I not been so much on my guard. She was also, put simply, extremely nice to be with. Perhaps she was the ultimate *femme fatale*. I slowed down my rate of ale consumption as I found I wanted to enjoy the evening. I was, however, determined to avoid getting fully ensnared. One trip to go for me and the lads and there was no way I was going to risk the Curse of the Chop Girl. So, I behaved with amazing propriety and like a true gentleman, which she seemed to appreciate even if she had expected otherwise.

It was a short distance back to the station, a mile or so, so I did the decent thing and walked her home. I assumed that she was a denizen of the Waafery, that sanctuary for all single aircraftwomen where males feared to tread. Eve told me no different so I thanked her for the very real pleasure of her company and wished her goodnight.

I mentioned none of this to Smithy or the other lads.

We then struck lucky. The following night we were sent on the final op of our tour but, rather than yet another blood-soaked sortie to the Ruhr with its promise of fiery death, we were sent on a mining trip. Dropping sea mines, known as 'Gardening', was almost as much the luck of the draw as bombing ops though generally with a higher chance of returning unscathed. The gods of war were smiling favourably as we were sent to an area in the Bay of Biscay where the enemy's radar coverage was more limited and his night fighters usually didn't bother to search for the occasional solo bomber. There was, naturally, still the risk of mechanical failure or foul weather but, on balance, we were appreciative of this of all tasks. It could have been far worse.

Eve was not on parachute duty, for which I was also grateful. I would have found it difficult not to acknowledge any greeting or flicker of recognition from her and I knew that Smithy would have noticed any interaction. His reaction would have been undoubtedly hostile, resulting in an unbearable tension which might easily have risked us all. One trip left and then ops would be behind us, we would go our separate ways and who knows what the future held. At least we would have a future. Keep smiling on us, oh gods, I thought. I had, I believed, kept my unspoken part of the bargain with fate and avoided a fatal embrace with the Chop Girl so I felt it would have been unsporting of Destiny to drop me in it now.

Destiny didn't let me down. The Gardening trip was flawless; the weather was calm and the moon hid obligingly behind some high-level cloud. The Luftwaffe even seemed to be on a night off; we certainly saw no other aircraft from the time we took off till our landing back at base five hours later.

As we taxied back to our dispersal and the pilots switched off the engines, we finally allowed ourselves the luxury of cheering, shouting and, in Ron's case, singing with joy. The song in question, was some Australian ditty the words of which have not stayed in my memory. After the months of tension, the sense of relief was the most powerful emotion I can recall. We had bought ourselves that most valuable, and taken-for-granted, of gifts: time. Time to live, time to love and time for enjoying every day. The ground crew were almost as ecstatic as we were; it had been a couple of months since a crew had last survived to the end of a full tour. From somewhere they had found six bottles of beer and these were shared around amongst us all. We had to cut short our celebrations for a short while as we had a somewhat perfunctory debrief to attend. For a Gardening sortie with no sight of the enemy this did not take long, and the Flight Lieutenant conducting the debrief was in no mind to interrogate us in too much depth.

Our flight commander told us it would probably be a few days before we found out where we were to be posted and what our new roles were to be. We would be split up as a crew unless we chose to volunteer for an immediate second tour. Experience was in short supply and we were apparently very welcome to stay with our squadron for the additional twenty ops that would constitute a second stint. We considered this for a couple of seconds before declining that wonderful and enticing opportunity.

We went our separate ways. Judy had managed to wangle some leave to coincide with Smithy's release from ops and they were last seen heading for the London train. The other lads packed their belongings with equal haste and I've never seen them to this day. Other crews we had seen complete a tour had enjoyed a riotous evening in the pub, swearing blind to stick together as a unit and live or die together. We were less cohesive; I think the recent stresses, together with the difference in rank across the crew meant that we were simply too weary once the immediate excitement had worn off. By the time we had got our collective breath back, it was too late.

I hadn't forgotten my WAAF friend; indeed, with time on my hands and the immediate threat of death seemingly removed, I regained a sense of perspective. Also, I didn't have Smithy's gloomy prognosis to contend with. I wanted to meet her again, I knew that much, and to see if there was a real and lasting spark between us. So instead of leaving the area and returning to my parents, on whom I was not desperately dependent, I booked a room above the White Knight. I could handle the raucous evenings as I could compensate by relaxed mornings in bed.

On my second night, Eve materialised in the bar. As before, I didn't notice her come into the pub as I leant against the bar, chatting to the barmaid and the regulars who were becoming almost like old friends. She was in the same seat when I looked round, alone once more. She smiled straight away when she saw me so I bought her half a pint of beer and went to join her. She didn't seem to mind the intrusion; in fact, she told me that she had hoped to find me again. I apologised for not having found a way of contacting her previously. She knew, she said, that we had finished our tour and had been disappointed at the thought that I had just left without seeing her.

Eve asked me my plans, to which I answered, with complete honesty, that I had none. I was awaiting my posting and had left word with our adjutant's office that I would be hanging around until the RAF decided what it would like me to do next. Meanwhile the landlord of the White Knight had offered me an excellent rate to stay for a couple of weeks, probably guessing that he would get the difference back over the counter of the bar.

'I can get a few days off if you'd like company.' The offer from Eve came out of the blue; it was something I hadn't even considered and now she had mentioned it the prospect was exciting indeed. Bear in mind that I had mentally talked myself out of my earlier worries about her being a jinx. We spent the rest of the evening in the bar and then agreed to do so the following evening by which time Eve would have organised a leave pass. We would agree how to pass the time once that happened.

Unusually for the RAF, matters seemed to be put in place swiftly for Eve, without the habitual bureaucracy and cussedness for which our organisation was rightly known. The following evening, Eve came in as promised, telling me that she had six days' leave. She didn't have a bag so I assumed that she would be returning to the Waafery each night. We could, perhaps, sort out a trip away in due course.

That evening there was a dance in the village hall which seemed like a good place to start. It went swimmingly for us and we drew closer, emotionally and then physically. To cut a long story short, it was a simple matter to smuggle Eve into my room above the pub. The passion was mutual and matters took the inevitable turn; it bothered me not one jot now that my tour had finished. I slept very well afterwards.

In the morning, there was no sign of her.

I spent a long day by myself, wondering about her apparent change of heart. Maybe, I thought, I had pushed things too far, too quickly, though Eve had seemed a willing, even eager, participant. I was sure that she had not been summoned back to the station, as no one would have known where to find her. Eventually, mystified and at a loose end, I went back to the station on the pretext of checking for news of my posting. Once past the Guard Room at the entrance, I went to the Parachute Section to see if she had had a sudden change of heart, only to be met by a total lack of help from the three aircraftwomen engaged in checking the packs for the night's ops. In fact, they had never heard of her, they told me. I realised that this was probably their habitual response to any love-struck airman who turned up asking after a specific girl. They probably had a repeat performance of such dramas daily. Get over it, seemed to be their less-than-helpful attitude.

Eve did turn up again that evening in the pub. She apologised and told me she had to get away and that it was nothing personal. I didn't mention having gone to the Parachute Section; I didn't want her to think I was hounding her. I was just glad that she was back and seeming to be as keen as ever to enjoy my company.

When she was absent again the following morning, I didn't know whether to accept this strange behaviour or to get hung up on it. I decided to bide my time and see if she came back to the pub that night. With two days of her leave gone, if we were going to share some real quality time we had better arrange a trip away pretty soon.

Sure enough, she was there in the bar at the usual time. I didn't want to spoil the moment so I was fairly gentle with her about her disappearance, but in the event, she didn't volunteer any information of use. I did broach the subject of a few days away, while she still had some leave left to take. Eve looked at me and I could see tears in her eyes. 'I can't go away at the moment; I can't tell you why but you need to trust me.' Then she brightened slightly as she added, 'I can be with you every night, though,' and gave me one of her radiant smiles.

We had another convivial evening and a very memorable night, then settled down to sleep. I was more restless than normal, still on edge in case Eve got up to leave. So, I was awake when she sat up in bed. Instinctively I kept my eyes closed and feigned sleep as she got out of bed and dressed without speaking. She kissed my forehead and left the room, descending the stairs as quietly as she could. I quickly put my own clothes on and followed her out of the pub cautiously. My insatiable curiosity meant I was willing to risk upsetting her, but I desperately wanted to know where she went. As I emerged from the yard of the pub I could see Eve a hundred yards or so along the high street, walking steadily but in no apparent rush. The sky was clear and there was a setting moon which helped me follow her. I felt furtive as I kept close to the building line lest she turn round. Eve evidently did not consider that she was being tailed and did not look back once.

I presumed that she would go to the Waafery so was surprised when she did not head for the airfield. Instead she walked the length of the village main street towards the parish church. By the time Eve reached the lychgate I had, with growing complacency, closed the distance to about twenty yards. When she entered the churchyard, I was not far behind and I could see her then, as she walked to the middle of the cluster of graves. And then she simply disappeared.

Fearing that Eve had slipped and fallen, I threw all caution to the wind and hurried to where I had last seen her. There was no sign of her anywhere. As I stood there, in the middle of what was now a deserted country churchyard in the dark hours before dawn, I noticed that the headstone on the grave by which I had last seen her was quite recent. Then, as I made out the stone's inscription in the moonlight, I suddenly doubted my own sanity.

'Eve Joyce Chandler', it read, with a date of death the previous year.

The vicar found me, apparently, when he came to open the church after breakfast. I have little recollection of the few hours that had passed since I last saw Eve, and discovered the grave with her name on it. The vicar thought I had been sleeping off a heavy night when he saw me hunched on a bench near the church door. However, as I recovered my senses, he realised that I had been in shock rather than drunk, and invited me to the vicarage for a warming cup of tea.

I asked the vicar what he knew of Eve, though without telling him of my own association with the woman.

'Ah, therein lies a tragic tale,' he told me. 'I buried the poor girl last year. She was from away but had moved here with her husband of a few months. A bomber boy, he was, like yourself. Eve joined the WAAF but was posted to another station. Her husband, like so many of your fellows, went missing eventually. His crew survived and one evaded capture and managed to get back here. He gave an account of Flight Lieutenant Chandler's heroism, staying at the controls while his crew baled out. Apparently his aircraft blew up shortly after the last of the crew got out so they are sure he was killed.

'Eve was beside herself with grief, and it was made worse by the knowledge that he had died alone. She was heard to say that she wished with all her heart she could get a new crew together for him so that he would have some mates with him to keep him company. No one thought much of it, as she was out of her mind at the time. She came back here and, one night, hung herself from the branch of a tree next to the airfield fence. She just wanted to be back with her husband.'

So, there you are. And here I am, not knowing what fate has in store for me. I will return to ops in due course, with another crew. It is most likely that the odds will beat me in the end, but they don't need the help of a Chop Girl to make that so.

I have stayed, for now, in my room above the White Knight; it's not as if I have anywhere else to go until my next posting comes through, which I expect will be any day now. I haven't seen Eve again, and I certainly haven't gone out looking for her.

Does Eve think that, at last, she brought a full crew together for her husband? She only needed a Wireless Operator to make it complete and maybe she thought I would fit the bill. I hope that she is now satisfied and won't go out looking for the souls of bomber boys to crew for him. Perhaps I have, at last, broken the Curse of the Chop Girl and no other airmen will be seduced into a premature departure from this life. God knows that their time is probably short enough.

On the other hand, she might be on the other side of the great divide waiting to see me when I turn up. I hope, in that case, that it will be a long time before we renew our acquaintance.

The original handwritten account, transcribed by the author and reproduced above, was in an exercise book collected by the Committee of Adjustment from the locker of Sergeant Jim Parkinson when he failed to return from the first operation of his second tour.

Return of the Brylcreem Boys

The lads and I do like to have a laugh.

It's the life, for want of a better word, that we lead, the mates, the freedom, the lack of responsibility. You would be envious of us if you saw the good times we have, the japes, the pranks and the wind-ups. Or perhaps you would look at us and tut your disapproval. Young men without a care in the world, you might think. Haven't they got anything better to do? It wasn't like that in your day we know that, but then it never was. You might even think we don't know there's a war on.

But we feel that we've earned the right to carry on like this, after what we've been through. You wouldn't want to go through what each and every one of us did. And, yes, we do know there's a bloody war on. It's how we got here, it made us the men we are, and it will be with us always, long after most of you have forgotten about it.

One day, maybe soon, perhaps a long time in the future, you will have to take the same journey we all did. I can only hope that when that awful day comes, your transition is less painful, less horrific and a lot more peaceful than it was for us.

We had no choice in the matter. We joined up with such enthusiasm, the innocence and confidence of youth getting the better of our barely-formed judgement. We wanted to do our bit, to defeat Hitler and protect our families. Above all, our mates were joining up too, and none of us wanted to be left out, let alone be thought a coward. Most of our mates joined the Army, which was easy. As long as you could stand up straight, hold a rifle and walk in a straight line, the pongoes would let you in. A few, more intrepid or just plain barmy, went into the Navy, presumably because they loved the thought of getting cold, wet and seasick.

Not us, though. We had more sense. Who wanted to go through the hell of the trenches, as our dads and uncles described their own experience twenty or so years earlier? We signed up for the Royal Air Force. Ours was to be a different kind of war; more modern, scientific, cleaner and more clinical. Above all it was to be glamorous. After the Battle of Britain all we wanted was to become fighter pilots. The girls would fall over themselves to be with us, every evening would be spent in the mess or the pub, drinking pints of ale and reliving the exploits of each exciting day, spent throwing our Spitfires around the clear blue skies above Dover. We tended to try to look the part even before we might get the chance to act it. Unlike the pongoes or the wet lot, we took considerable pride in our appearance, unusually perhaps for lads our age. We wanted to be recognised as the Brylcreem Boys, so-called for the gel we plastered into our hair.

It didn't work out like that but by the time we knew what the RAF had planned, it was too late. You can't just change your mind and choose a cushier option, the awareness of how damned dangerous our job would be was drip-fed to us. It wasn't the cramped, cold, quarters or the dreadful food at the Initial Training Wing; that time didn't last very long. It wasn't even the dicey voyage on a requisitioned passenger liner, racing across the stormy ocean, trying to outpace the lurking U-boats. That was over soon enough, four days each way, and anyway it served to convince us that those who had joined the Navy must have needed their heads examining.

The unwelcome news started in basic flying training in the vastness of Canada. Every so often one or more members of the course would pile into the ground and that was that. Plenty of guts, but no glory for them. But we knew it wouldn't happen to us. And we were right, most of us. We left them there, too, and for all I know they are there still, while we made it back to England. Home to us all; by birth to most, by adoption to the rest, and for eternity for us all.

We were joined there by the lads from the rest of the Empire; the Canadians made the journey over the Atlantic with us, along with a sprinkling of Yanks who couldn't be bothered to wait for Uncle Sam to join the festivities. The Aussies and the Kiwis, along with South Africans, Rhodesians, Indians and West Indians, made their separate way to the dank, rain-sodden and downright miserable place that we had sworn on our lives to defend. We were, eventually, all in it together.

Our training, from initial recruitment to joining what for most of us turned out to be our first and only operational squadron, took about two years. We tended to be in our late teens or early twenties when we applied and our average age when we started ops was twenty-two. I was eighteen when I joined up, and twenty when I started my tour. Not a great age, in the scheme of things, but inside our heads we were old beyond our years, and worldly-wise. And we certainly saw and experienced many sights, sounds and emotions that the rest of you have never, should never, be privy to. Like the sudden, violent, nasty fiery deaths of so many of our mates, taken in the middle of the night as they flew alongside us. We tried to do what we could to avoid their fate, and to an extent we succeeded, for a short while. Your luck can only last so long, however, so we lived for the moment and clung to the still-undashed hope that it would always be someone else, never ourselves. 'So far, so good,' was our daily mantra.

It was that hope that carried us through; that, and the knowledge that we were doing our duty. Not to mention the fact that we were in the forces, had bought the ticket so had no choice but to go for the ride. The alternative was the shame and ignominy of being branded 'LMF', Lack of Moral Fibre. For such poor individuals came the stigma of being cast out of the gang as a coward. The fact we were volunteers to a man counted for nothing with the powers-that-be. We couldn't un-volunteer; if they let anyone get away with that, we would start a stampede because, by now, we realised that the job was a one-way ticket to oblivion for most of us. But we carried on; it was our job and our mates and so we kept going to war. Most of us came back each time, but gradually the familiar faces disappeared. But still we clung to the belief that it was always him, never me. Until it really was our turn.

I am sure you are wondering what is the point of my ramblings on behalf of myself and those with whom I am spending what seems like an eternity? Well, you may well have had cause to wonder what became of us, and where we have gone. In some cases, you may have cause to believe that we never went away. Perhaps I can shed some light on the situation.

You see, many of us have never truly moved on. We had become used to our environment and to the company we were keeping. Despite the tension, the stress and the gut-wrenching fear when we were on ops, or when we paused for thought between flights, mostly we were having an absolutely wizard time. We are young men, in a predominantly young society, working and playing hard. It was just like being a rugby club playing games away every day. There was no shortage of beer. There was, admittedly, a dearth of women when we were on the station but enough in the pubs and in town to keep us motivated. We were all lads together for the rest of the time. Think back to when you were twenty, if indeed you have been that age. You've got a job, plenty of chums and your accommodation and food are all provided. Would you have had a care in the world if that was you? But what made it different was that fear and tension that I alluded to earlier. It was emotional intensity to a very high degree, whether the highs of a beer session when we were stood down, or the lows of dreading imminent death. Neither are the sort of thing that would fade from your memory, and we can't shake them off now.

Have you ever wondered why there are so many ghost stories linked to the air war against Germany? Consider the numbers: by the time the war ended, for you at least, the RAF had lost about seventy thousand of us, mostly from Bomber Command. But in the scheme of things, that is pretty small beer. Where are the other ghosts? Farmers, train drivers, builders, chartered accountants? I mean, everybody has to die eventually so you would think the world would be awash with the spirits of the departed. But apart from the legends of headless horsemen, or wraiths wandering around stately homes moaning and wailing, where is everybody?

Maybe we didn't know how to die properly. Just as we lived every minute, getting the most out of each experience as if it was our last, perhaps we are imprinted too firmly in the folk memory to be able to let go. It's a mystery to us as well, by the way, as we have no way of knowing what it was like for everyone else. I think that because we lived and died with so much greater intensity than other mortals, that we have tended to hang around for longer. We've got our pals with us so maybe that binds us here and to each other as well.

Please bear with me while I tell you what we went through. I can't speak for all of us as we found many different ways to die. We were, variously, torn apart by cannon shells or flak, shot by machine gun bullets, or blown to pieces in an instant when our bomber exploded. Sometimes we bled slowly to death from our wounds, alone in our assigned position or, if we were lucky, on the crew bunk tended by a crew-mate and given morphine to kill the pain. Sometimes we even made it back to England before succumbing to our wounds and injuries. We fell from a great height trailing the remnants of a burnt or shredded parachute, we were trapped by g-forces inside a plummeting aeroplane and pulverised when it smashed itself and us at high speed into the ground, which is what happened to me. Worst of all, from what I am told, was when we were consumed by fire.

I won't bore you with the details of my ops, even of the one when my number came up and I got The Chop, as we glibly referred to it. If you prefer, I went for a Burton. The RAF posted me as 'Missing on operations' initially and then, after a decent period, 'Missing, Believed Killed'. I don't know if they ever found me, even to this day. Maybe I'm still, and will always be, Missing. Even I don't know where I am. I do know I was over the Ruhr when my turn came, Happy Valley. Lots of fighters, then lots of flak. Something hit us from underneath, I don't know what but it's a fair bet it was made in Germany. Probably Krupps of Essen, which would be an irony as that was what we were trying to bomb at the time. I was the wireless operator / air gunner and the aeroplane, a Halifax bomber which rejoiced in the code O-Orange, decided that it didn't want to play any longer. It was very dark, and I found myself pinned against the side of the fuselage as the Halibag went into a terminal spin. I can't tell you anything more than that, of any substance. I was too stunned and frightened to have coherent thoughts about what was happening, was about to happen, or what I was leaving behind. It did seem to take a hell of a long time for things to stop happening but eventually they did just that. It came to an end with a massive blow which knocked me senseless. In fairness, it didn't actually hurt. You know when you hit your thumb with a hammer? You realise what you've just done but it takes a split second for your thumb to alert its nerves and get them to let you brain know what's occurred? Then it hurts like billy-oh but you have that brief period before the pain sets in. Well, it's like that but in a much bigger way. You know something spectacular has just happened but, in the split second before your brain gets its act together and decides which bit hurts most, you die. You don't feel a thing. I can assure that is absolutely true, if it is of any comfort.

And then, what? Well, the Afterlife wasn't what I had been led to believe. No sign of Jesus, that's for sure. Maybe he doesn't know there's a war on either. When I regained my wits, I was back at RAF Elliston, the base from which I had departed a few short hours earlier. I was standing in the room we used for debriefing by the intelligence wallahs. I was a bit disorientated, to say the least. Initially I thought I must have had a bang on the head and that the trip home had been a complete blur. I could see plenty going on around me, but I wasn't part of it nor it of me. It was like when you get really drunk, to the point that things seem to be happening around you and you are always half a second behind events. At least I didn't have any trouble standing upright on this occasion.

The people around me were insubstantial, they didn't seem to notice me and when I tried to talk to anyone I got no response or even an acknowledgement. I saw another WOP from another crew whom I knew reasonably well, at least in passing, so I greeted him with a cordial 'Hello, old boy.' He ignored my greeting even though we were face to face. I tried tap him on the shoulder and my hand just passed through him, as if he wasn't there. That did concern me and a chill ran down my spine as I thought I was seeing a ghost. Then, looking around me at the host of other figures moving around perfectly normally and getting on with their post-flight business, it dawned on me that, just maybe, it was me, not my erstwhile comrades, that was the ethereal form drifting around at a loose end. I desperately attempted to make contact with others, reaching out to no tangible effect; speaking then shouting at them. Nothing at all, no reply nor even a flicker of acknowledgement, was offered in return so I sat down on a chair in a row at the back of the room, where we would normally wait for the intel bods to get around to debriefing our crew. On this occasion, the familiar chair did its bit in supporting me.

I knew I needed to determine the state of my vitality or, alternatively, mortality. I would feel a right chump if I was wrong; at the very least my colleagues would assume that I'd lost my marbles whilst at worst the MO, not to mention the Flight and Squadron Commanders, would assume that this was an extreme case of lead-swinging and brand me LMF, writing me off as a coward. Perhaps you can understand why I needed to establish the truth, no matter how unpalatable it might prove. Therefore, I decided to walk through the nearest wall. That's what ghosts do, isn't it?

It should have been as simple as that. I got off my seat, turned to the wall behind me, took two steps and crashed straight into the damned thing. It didn't hurt, but I couldn't get through it. 'Bang goes that theory,' I thought. Maybe I wasn't dead after all, but I needed to find out for certain. I went to the door and opened it, stepping out into the corridor, into the path of two NCOs who passed through me without a break in their stride. That was concerning, to put it mildly. Then I had a brainwave. I remembered that, whilst at school, I had read an anthology of ghost stories, and it had mentioned that vampires didn't have reflections. I was not quite sure whether that also applied to ghosts, as the authors had been a bit evasive on that issue, but thought I might as well put it to the test. I went to the Officers' Mess, which had a suitably large and ornate mirror behind the bar. At the time, I went in the place was deserted, which was probably for the best as I felt a bit self-conscious at the prospect of preening in a mirror and then asking anyone present if they could see me. It simply wasn't the sort of thing a chap did.

When I looked in the mirror, there was no one returning my stare.

That convinced me I was dead. Unless I woke up from this rather vivid dream, I was a goner. I was, quite literally, mortified.

Bloody hell.

Even that thought immediately became irrelevant. Just as there were no Pearly Gates, ethereal folk with haloes and harps, or an old bearded chap trying to repel boarders, there was no sign of an eternal furnace either. That was a relief. I thought, with a tinge of guilt that was probably superfluous now, of my various sins which, though minor in the scheme of things, were probably more numerous than would have enhanced my good name. If you overlooked the small matter of carpet-bombing a few towns in Germany, though even that was probably excusable under the prevailing circumstances.

On the other hand, it occurred to me that I would probably now spend the rest of eternity in the Royal Air Force. That was a dismal prospect, with due respect to that august organisation, as I had always imagined that one day the war would end and I might go and find a more lucrative and less intrusive way of earning a living.

Amazingly I still felt alive, which probably sounds ridiculous. I had the same sense of self, that mysterious feeling of consciousness that becomes more unfathomable the more you pause to think about it. I was still here, in my former surroundings; it was just that no one, and nothing, else seemed to be aware of me.

Returning to the briefing room, I stood in the path of a few chaps, waiting until some other crewmen had walked through me, just to see if I was still dead, which I was. There was no sign of a return to the land of the living. Someone else was now sitting in what I thought was my chair and I was understandably reluctant to sit in his lap, not that he would have noticed.

I realised I'd better get used to my new state; I presumed that I was going to be dead for rather a long time. Rather than sadness, after the initial shock wore off, I felt annoyed that I had been chopped. The Hun had got the better of me and I was nearly through my tour. Twenty-eight bloody ops, plus the delivery of a twenty-ninth bomb load on our final sortie, that's what the RAF got for two years of training and Christ alone knew how much investment. Oh well, tough, I concluded. They couldn't exactly put it on my Mess bill, though I expect they would insist on settling that out of my next and final pay. It was particularly galling that we had this and one more op to complete before our six months respite. Early in the tour we knew that our chances were not good, putting it mildly. If we survived this tour, the chances of making it through a second were equally slim, though the RAF did the decent thing and only expected another twenty from us. But once we passed twenty-five, we began to hope. Only another five, four, three then two… Except we never got beyond that.

It was going to take a bit of getting used to. Why, I wondered, did I go back to base? Not that I had been given any choice in the matter but I suppose it was, and still is, very familiar, which was a tremendous comfort under the circumstances. Maybe there is an emotional tie that hauled us back there and, in any case, it was better than mooching around some godforsaken part of the Third Reich for the rest of time. That was something to be grateful for. I'd never actually been to Germany until I collided with it at about 450 knots, so I would hate to be stuck there for ever. I couldn't speak German in any case, and their ghosts probably wouldn't exactly welcome me with open arms.

At first, I thought I was alone, and hoped that the other lads had escaped, but after a while hanging around the debriefing room with no one bothering to ask me what I could contribute to the sum of human knowledge, I went off to mooch around the Station. Almost as soon as I had drifted into the room I shared with Frank, our bomb aimer, I saw him standing there, large and solid as life. He saw me too, as he immediately said 'Peter, old boy, I presume you didn't make it either'.

'Didn't stand a chance, old chap. At least it was damned quick, and didn't hurt. What happened to the others?'

'Not sure. I would be surprised if any of us made it.' We compared notes on being dead, in the same matter of fact tone as we did when debriefing any op or exercise. Frank had similarly found everything going black and then found himself back here. Death seemed to be somewhat consistent; however, when you consider that we were being blasted off our former mortal coil in industrial quantities, maybe even the Grim Reaper had reached the limit of his creativity in dragging us through the veil.

'Might as well have a wander around and see if they've turned up,' I said eventually, having exhausted our thoughts on our new circumstances. We left the room and checked the Officer's Mess, where our pilot and navigator, Dickie and Harry respectively, were standing by the bar looking a bit downcast. There was no one to serve them, after all, as the bar itself was shut. There didn't seem to be any provision for booze where we were now, which seemed to be a bit of a blunder by the Almighty, in our view. Or maybe some divine smart alec decided that this would be our idea of hell. In that case, there would probably be no decent nosh and no popsies either.

The other three lads were NCOs, so, in their former lives, had not been welcomed anywhere near the salubrious environs of the Officers' Mess. We went to find them; lesser mortals they might have been in the eyes of the RAF establishment but they were our mates, and anyway they weren't mortals any longer. None of us were. They were sitting on their beds in the miserable Nissen hut that had served as their home for these past few weeks. I would like them to have got out of the prang in one piece, as I'm not selfish. They could have told people what had happened to us and maybe someone would have found the wreckage of the plane and given those who didn't make it the chance to get a decent burial, somewhere for our families to visit us.

We could see the faint figures of the living moving around us, carrying on their daily business, but we certainly couldn't interact with them. Not just then, anyway. We had to learn how to do that and there was no one to teach us at first. But, what the heck? We had time on our hands and there was nobody telling us what to do the whole time; no station duties, no jankers, no mindless cleaning, painting or aimless square-bashing. It's like every day is a holiday. We don't know we're born.

There were several other lads in our situation; I wouldn't call it a predicament as that would suggest that there was a way out of it but for us there wasn't. Some of them I recognised as having gone missing in the few weeks we'd spent with the squadron. We weren't close friends with anyone on other crews. There wasn't time to get to know them as the chop rate was pretty horrific at that point, as we'd found out. You saw the chaps in your own trade; in my case the wireless operators who would still be required to focus on improving our skills when we weren't in the air putting it all into practice. But we never really socialised with them. We were all just faces in the Mess or the briefing room, uniformed figures and bods encumbered in flying kit as we gathered in the locker room before and after every flight. In our case, though, the meetings before flights outnumbered those after by one. We only really knew, and gave a hoot about, those on our own crew and no one else seemed particularly bothered about us. Certainly, the remaining personnel on the station seemed to be unburdened by grief at our loss as they went about their daily routine.

There were many others who weren't there, even though they were known to have bought it. None of those who'd crashed in training flights in our time were present, nor many of those whose aircraft had been seen to pile in en route to or from the target. It was a mystery to us. We did discuss it as we hung around the place. We decided that those of us left simply hadn't been discovered yet. That matters, you see, to us as much as to our families, and it's another possible reason why there are so many of us still here. More than twenty thousand of us have no known grave, in fact, or so I gather. Maybe that's why some of us do eventually disappear, even from here. They do get found, and have a decent send off, albeit several years or decades later, and off they go. It's just not happened to me yet.

Pretty soon, we all seemed to be resigned to our fate, insofar as we knew what it was. Being young lads at heart, it wasn't long before we started making the most of things. After all that was what we'd been doing since joining up. Traveling in our new dimension was an absolute piece of cake. If you thought about somewhere with a sincere sense of longing to go there, you just went. No tickets, no discomfort or queueing; in wartime England that was a very welcome change. Having found out that I could go home at will, and return, I told the lads and we all had a go. This entailed a good bit of investigation to test the limits, so we went for quick trips out to all the places we had loved previously. Even Dickie, who hailed from Australia, found that he could, in no time at all, be lurking invisibly in the bar of his favourite Sydney pub.

The only constraint was that you couldn't go somewhere unless you really had been there in your earthly life. This wasn't too much of an inconvenience and it spared us the ordeal of accidentally going to Germany, a country unknown to the others as well as to me, at surface level. As a crew, we struggled to find somewhere we had all visited outside the rather unadventurous option of our training stations. Then we remembered, shortly after crewing up at the Heavy Conversion Unit, we had a 48-hour pass. Too short for a long trip home, or the relative excitement of London, we had gone as a group to York, which had been a short bus ride away from the base.

We thought our way to a spot on the walls, just behind York Minster. Last time we were there it had been an uncommonly pleasant and warm couple of spring days and we had lounged on a small terrace which seemed to mark one corner of the fortifications. Dickie had asked a passing WAAF to take a photograph of us, with the alluring promise of a date with him that evening. She had decided to forego that particular treat because, she told him, her pass ran out at 1800 hours, but she took the picture anyway. Somehow, he had bribed, threatened or cajoled the Station Photographic Section to run off a copy each for us to post home. I was glad he'd done that, and perhaps that is why the wall terrace was worthy of an enduring place in our affection.

A very agreeable time we had, too. It felt as warm as when we had been there previously, so we did what we now did so well; absolutely nothing. We lounged around, once again, chatting and generally winding each other up. One benefit of being incorporeal was that we could leap off the battlements without getting hurt. That entertained us for a while. Then we thought of going to a pub we had also visited last time out, which worked very well as we were back there in an instant. Unfortunately, for us there was no way of enjoying a real pint, so that rather defeated the object. However, once we thought hard enough about the beer we had consumed we found that we could all recreate the experience in our memory and that had to suffice. It dawned on me that what we could do now was limited only by our memories of our time on Earth. That was fine for those of us who had led an adventurous life but, I considered, it must get a bit dreary if all you had ever done was go to a strict school or you'd been brought up in an orphanage.

I went home at one point, quite early on. There was no one to issue me a leave pass so I just cleared off; I would deal with the consequences on my return, if there were to be any. I was confident that there wouldn't, not least because the RAF Police and the Adjutant never took to the air so hadn't got around to dying yet.

My spot of impromptu leave was not the best move, perhaps, as the atmosphere at my parent's home was completely different to the station. My mother was clearly in mourning and my father was even more morose than I had known him at his miserable best. God, I had taken them for granted when I was them. I could see now that they had truly loved me and were devastated at my loss.

Worst of all was my kid brother. He had just turned fifteen, joined the new Air Training Corps and was hell-bent on following me into the RAF. What could possibly go wrong? We had always been friends as well as brothers, the age difference of five years becoming increasingly irrelevant as we grew up. It was very difficult to stand next to him and see him breaking his heart. I knew I didn't want him to go through the hell on earth that was ops, let alone the cataclysmic transition I had just endured, but I couldn't think what I could do to stop him. I now knew that, if the worst came to the worst, there was something beyond death to look forward to. In the meantime, I would try and find a way to keep an eye on him, if the war went on that long. I had seen enough so I went back to the Station.

We did have flying in common, so we spent a while working out how we could still do that. Once again, though, it was as simple as discussing which event we wanted to recall, then thinking our way through it. It seemed to work and we even managed to conjure up O-Orange and took her out for a spin. The familiarity of being back inside our Hallie was immensely comforting, at least whilst we were floating around the local flying area, so we did that quite a bit. We could recreate sorties with amazing accuracy after a bit of practice. To us it became almost as real as it had always been, as well as a lot more practical. We didn't have to wait our turn to take-off or land; at an early stage, we found that we could simply move through any obstacles in our path, airborne or on the ground. In fact, it was usually them moving through us; at first, we didn't want to get things badly wrong and it went totally against the grain to aim our aeroplane at another bomber. That just came with practice.

It was mingling with obstacles in the real world, whilst cavorting around in O-Orange, that started to make more sense to us. Just as the things we were used to from before were tangible, like the briefing room wall, the chair and O-Orange, anything new was as ethereal to us as we must have been to those who still existed in the physical world. An RAF station in war time was in constant flux, with old buildings being demolished and new ones put up the whole time. To us, it was still the old structures that formed the boundaries of our world; new walls, doors and all the rest of the material world were far more nebulous and we discovered we could move through at will.

Strange though it may seem, our world remained constant and seemed very real; all the old barriers were in the same place and we could not walk through the walls now any more than we could previously. Conversely, the new buildings that appeared all over the airfield, and walls and partitions that were moved, appeared vague and transparent to us, and were no obstacle to our progress. A pattern was, by now, becoming apparent. Our memories were our new reality and this included other lads we now recognised as ghosts, knowing that they had failed to return from raids before our own demise. Every so often we were joined by fresh faces, including several we recognised from our time alive, though the number of recognisable new arrivals decreased as time went on. That was simply because familiar bods were replaced with people we didn't know as they went missing or, more rarely, completed their tour of ops and left.

Time had no real meaning to us now; we didn't have to keep to any kind of schedule and could come and go as we pleased. We were always there or thereabouts; even when we went off on a periodic visit, alone or in company, we found we would inevitably gravitate back to the base. It was, quite literally, our old haunt. The lack of meaningful activity, so hated by the powers-that-be in any service organisation, did mean that we were always at a loose end, sometimes to the extent that we found ourselves overwhelmed by boredom. It did cross my mind that, with an eternity to spend hanging around the place, this might get worse and that I would find myself driven up the wall by a monotonous and purposeless existence, assuming I still existed at all.

Bored lads in their early twenties are never going to be the epitome of peace and tranquillity, so I was determined to keep myself and my colleagues entertained. In the Officers' Mess, such downtime as we had on breaks between ops, usually caused by days of thick fog smothering the airfield, would result in an outbreak of high spirits, always fuelled by the cheap, if watery, beer that was available to us in prodigious quantities. Mess rugby was a popular, and exceedingly raucous, pastime, usually resulting in a hefty bill to be shared subsequently by the participants to pay for the damage; how we didn't manage to kill any of our colleagues was a mystery in itself. As a creative diversion on one occasion, when the Wing Co had flown to High Wycombe for a conference, a few of my colleagues had carefully dismantled his prized Austin Seven motor car, brought it into the Mess and reassembled it precariously on top of the grand piano, a splendid instrument which could, in naval service, have served as a small aircraft carrier. In fairness the boss, on his return, saw the funny side, though he demanded an apology to the Mess Committee from the miscreants because of the oil which dripped from the badly-reassembled engine onto the piano and the carpet.

We were still amenable to such pranks; being dead doesn't mean you lose your sense of humour. We could relive them in our shared memories, and had many evenings of enjoyment in the Mess with our officer colleagues re-running such japes. As the NCOs hadn't experienced such activities they could not now take part but they did manage to relive old times in the Sergeants' Mess with their recently-departed colleagues.

I was relaxing with another denizen of the Officers' Mess, a pilot who had introduced himself when we first met as Gordon Postlethwaite. He was quite tall for a bomber pilot and sported a fine handlebar moustache. Gordon had copped a packet a couple of months earlier than my crew, bringing a damaged Lanc back from the Ruhr. Prior to that he had been based at this very airfield and completed a tour on Whitleys, so he described the base, without a trace of irony, as his spiritual home. One evening he regaled me with his account of frightening the wits out of a couple of members of the still-alive brigade, as we referred to the ghostly forms of the mortals moving in our midst.

'I was, for some strange reason, dwelling on how Bert, my nav, and I would sit in the NAAFI on days when weren't on ops. It was warmer in there than the Nissen hut and there was always a brew on. So, I found myself back there, like we do, but no navigator. I haven't seen him since I got the chop, so I was on my own. There were a few other bods lurking around, no one on our side of the fence, and they didn't notice me at first. Anyway, I got to thinking about how they would be feeling, all the stress and worry about what lay ahead, and it all came back to me what had gone through my own mind when Bert and I were actually there. It was crystal clear for a few moments, really felt like I was back there. I glanced over to the counter and saw the two ladies behind the counter, you'll know them, Gladys and Ethel, staring at me. They looked terrified, not that I'd done anything to frighten them. I knew them to speak to when I was here properly, and they knew me. So, Gladys says to Ethel, "Strike a light, Eth, that bloke don't half look like Gordon Postlethwaite." And Ethel says, "He does that, but I heard Gordon caught it a few weeks back. Maybe it's his brother." That broke my train of thought and I must have disappeared, as Ethel then said, "Blimey Glad, he's vanished." The two char dispensers gawped at me for a few seconds, evidently no longer able to see me, before pouring themselves a cup of tea and hot footing it into the kitchen.

I didn't like the thought of frightening them, so waited a few days before trying it again.'

'Does it work every time then?' I was keen to know.

'Only in certain places, for some reason. I can go to any place I can remember, like we all can, I imagine. But the only places I can be visible are those where I can get a very strong sense of my previous emotions.'

'Sounds like a barrel of laughs,' I commented. 'Did you try it again, then?'

'Like I said, I didn't feel too cocky about it that first time, especially since Glad and Ethel had been real treasures for me before I left. I thought I'd pick another group for my next experiment. I went to see some fitters.'

Our groundcrew, which comprised a motley collection of tradesmen who were experts in the magical arts of airframe and engine maintenance, electrics and the whizzo secret radio equipment we carried around, were a tough bunch. They had to be; they worked, for the most part, outside in the foul weather for which Yorkshire was rightly famous. Toiling for long hours, they had none of the perks of aircrew so had to put up with all the bull that came from being Other Ranks in the Old Boys Club that was the Royal Air Force. As a result, their personalities were cynical and insensitive to emotion to the same degree as their dedication and motivation in their work. They were the salt of the Earth and not a man amongst them would allow himself to show a flicker of apprehension. A more appropriate bunch for a ghostly visit would be hard to conjure up.

Gordon continued, 'I know I used to get a touch of the jitters when I got to dispersal before an op, and that started to affect me before any flight, in fact. It was just being there, knowing what could so easily happen. I don't think it ever showed; my crew never mentioned it or even gave me an inkling that they had noticed, but I knew how I felt. I went out to our old pan and found another plane there; one of yours, a Halifax, not a Whitley like we had when I was here. I'd never been in a Halifax so I couldn't put myself inside it now, but it didn't matter. I just stood at the edge of the pan at first, like I used to with my lads before the off. There were a couple of erks working on one of the engines, but they were intent on their job, ensuring whoever took her up next would have at least one engine working properly. Anyway, I waited a few minutes and then decided to see what was happening on the other side of the plane, so I walked in front of her, past the two fitters. I'd got my flying kit on, as that was what I was always wearing out there, and one of them looked down to me and shouted, 'I wouldn't bother hanging around for this one, we'll be three or four hours yet', so he'd obviously seen me. Then he just got on with his work.'

'He didn't drop his spanner, or fall off the wing then?' I wanted to know.

'No, he must have thought I was just another pilot wanting to get on with his flight test. When you think about it, it must seem to them like we're always hanging around waiting for something to fly, like we've got nothing better to do. He probably wouldn't have recognised me in any case, even if he was close enough to get a good look. So, he's seen a ghost and didn't even know it.'

'Probably just as well that you didn't frighten him off; that engine would never have been fixed.'

'Yes, well, it would have been for the best,' Gordon replied after a brief pause. 'They went off on a raid that night and didn't come back, poor sods. I just hope I didn't bring the chopper down on them. It would be nice if a few of our mates could make it through this lot.'

'I can't see how that would have been your fault,' I told him. 'You had no way of knowing what was going to happen, did you? I mean, it's not as if you put a curse on them and the crew wasn't even out there with you. Have you been back out there again?'

Gordon told me he hadn't, adding, 'I suppose it makes little difference; most of us get the Chop sooner or later. We're proof of that. Tell you what, old boy, why don't we both give it a go.' He gave the matter a few moments more thought before continuing, 'If we take a saunter round the airfield, there might be a dispersal we both used and we can try and show ourselves there. Then all we've got to do is wait until there's a flap on and we can try to put in an appearance, then hang around till they all come back. If our lot go for a Burton we'll know not to do it again.'

This seemed to me to be far too good a wheeze to pass up, so I agreed to try it. For me, my most intense emotions had been on returning from ops, especially when the engines were shut down, we gathered our kit and clambered out of that pungent metal tube in which we had been incarcerated for the previous few hours. By that time, the adrenaline was starting to wear off and I would be feeling a mixture of relief that I had survived along with the aftershock of whatever close shaves we had experienced. There would also be an awareness, which. I would hardly dare acknowledge, that another of my intended thirty ops could be chalked off. I wondered if what Gordon had said about the intensity of his emotions determining where he could materialise applied to relief and joy as well as apprehension. I decided to try.

Gordon and I took a prolonged walking tour of the airfield. In our time there, we seemed to have used most of the dispersals, so could visit them. The few that I had never used, I simply couldn't get on to, though I could see Gordon clearly in the middle of the concrete circles that he had been on in the living past. He told me had experienced the same for my old dispersals. There were quite a number, though, that we had evidently both operated from. That part of the mission having been successfully accomplished, we repaired to the bar.

A day or so later there must have been another operation taking place back in the real world as the vague and insubstantial forms of the living were scurrying around in the way that was still so familiar. Gordon and I went back out onto the airfield and it was apparent that this was a maximum effort for the squadron, with an abundance of the angular dark Halifax bombers being checked over, fuelled and bombed up. We chose one of our mutual pans which was, by fate or coincidence, now the home to another O-Orange, the plane having been drafted in to replace her earlier namesake which was now, I presumed, at the bottom of a crater in Germany along with what was left of me. I sincerely hoped that I was right, and that we were not condemning the new O-Orange to a similar demise.

'How do I do this, then?' I asked Gordon.

'Think back to when you were here before. I mean, really focus on how you felt,' he told me.

The last time I could remember using that particular dispersal had been quite memorable, once I concentrated on the matter. We had paid a visit to Duisburg, uninvited as usual, an experience which the Hun had decided to make as unpleasant for us as it was for him. Our attempts to hoodwink the Luftwaffe into thinking we were going somewhere else had only worked up to a point and there were a fair number of night fighters trying to spoil the party. One such had bounced us and had a couple of goes at shooting us down before being driven off by the gunners. The skipper had put in some reasonably enthusiastic corkscrews in a valiant effort to lose our potential assassin and these had paid off. The plane looked like a colander when we landed and I had been even more than usually delighted to reach terra firma in East Yorkshire.

The emotion came flooding back to me and my senses, which by now I had become accustomed to as dulled, returned in all their former glory. I was back there. The sounds of a bomber squadron going about its deadly business were all around me, with a clarity all the greater for its prolonged absence. The colours of the grass and the sky were vibrant and the scent of the grass, mixed with the less rural smells of petrol, oil and exhaust fumes, were of greater intensity than I remembered them. Perhaps I had grown so used to all these that I had taken them for granted and my senses had stopped bothering with them. It was good to be back, however briefly.

Gordon was with me so we mooched around the dispersal watching the ground crew display their considerable skills at getting a front-line bomber ready for the off. I was somewhat startled, I must admit, when a passing erk, who evidently hailed from the East End of London, uttered to me as he passed, ‘Blimey guvnor, you’re a tad early ain’tcha?’ Those were his words, cliched or not. I’m sure no disrespect to rank was intended; after all my bulky flying clothing bore no insignia of rank on its rather dull and understated exterior. Gordon had been right; we could become visible.

Being young lads at heart, of course, we couldn't leave it at that, so decided to hang around and wave the crew off. Keeping focussed for that length of time, in order to remain visible, would have entailed a significant mental effort, and my powers of concentration weren't up to that, not yet anyway, so we faded from sight for a while. It was, somewhat perversely, quite pleasant to be back in an environment that we knew so well, even if it had been a time of nervous apprehension that sometimes bordered on dread. I certainly hadn't been back to monitor the squadron's activities since my return; as a crew, we decided it was far more fun going somewhere more relaxing.

To be honest, I wasn't even sure how much time had elapsed since I had formed part of a dent in the Third Reich, as we had no way of telling the time. I still had my Service-issue wristwatch, but it only ever showed the time to be twenty-eight minutes past two, which I realised was the time we had crashed. I had to be acutely aware of the time whilst on ops, as I had to tune into the Group frequency every quarter of an hour to pick up a code for the log. That would show the bosses that I had been paying attention and not gone to sleep or nipped back to the rear turret for a game of snap with the gunners. It could have been a few days but, then again, some weeks might well have elapsed. Certainly, there were very few familiar faces amongst the rather insubstantial forms that moved among us. We, however, were unchanged over time. At least the aircraft type hadn't changed, though some individual planes presumably still failed to materialise in the dawn after a raid, and were replaced by newer models.

Gordon and I had another sortie around the airfield. My senses were, I realised nowhere near as acute when I was not visible, but it was still quite pleasant. Even so, we managed to get a bit bored and decided to attend the briefing, just for old time's sake. This was a bit of a lark for us, as we didn't have to put up with all the security bull that descended on the station when ops were on. We could still go where liked, whenever we wanted. It would have given us a considerable sense of freedom had it not been for the circumstances in which we found ourselves.

We drifted into the room, just late enough to have earned a bollocking had we been on the earthly side of the divide. The squadron CO, secretly known to us as Groundbound as he rarely took to the air nowadays, had taken his place at the front of the room. After graciously allowing the assembled aircrew to sit down, he then said, with all the faux bonhomie he could muster, 'Gentlemen, you may smoke'. The chaps didn't need telling twice and the familiar blue fug began to fill the room as all concerned began to fill their lungs with the by-products of tobacco they had managed to lay their hands on. It was welcome, and it was good for them, or so the medical profession told us.

Groundbound, whom I remembered as an officious and over-promoted twerp, apparently laboured under the misapprehension that he was a respected leader of men. He had a taste for theatrical flamboyance; indeed, it was known that he had been an enthusiastic amateur actor before the war and he had attempted to engage our enthusiasm in establishing concert parties on the station when we weren't flying or doing anything else that might constitute a return on our service pay. He was wasting his time as the enthusiasm we had left was woefully short of the requisite level. With a flourish, the sometime thespian grasped the cord which drew back the curtains over a large map of Europe. By large, I mean it covered almost the entire back wall of the room. The map extended from the Atlantic Ocean in the West well into Poland in the East. I don't know how Groundbound would have managed if he'd decided we needed to bomb Moscow; maybe he would have extended the chart into the adjoining Nissen hut. Perhaps it was just as well that the Halifax lacked the range to fly out of the window, on that scale anyway. However, if Ireland had decided to throw in its lot with Hitler we would have turned left instead of right and that side of the map, virtually pristine to date, would have become a bit busier.

'Gentlemen,' announced Groundbound, once again, as he pulled the cord and the curtains opened. 'Your target for tonight is…' As the curtains revealed the ribbons stretching across the lower part of the North Sea, thence over Holland into Germany, an audible groan was emitted from the hundred or so men who, unlike Groundbound, would have to trace their path in the sky.

'…Essen.'

Groundbound's authoritative pronouncement was rather indistinct; in fact it was almost drowned out by a particularly heartfelt 'Oh, Jesus fucking wept…' in a strong Australian accent.

A fellow Aussie chipped in, 'I'm bored stiff with going to bloody Essen, mate, can't we go somewhere else?'

'Now then, gentlemen, it's nothing you haven't handled before,' was Groundbound's retort, his face becoming pale and his delivery more staccato as he became more annoyed at what he would undoubtedly, and correctly, discern to be an outbreak of insubordination.

One of our antipodean chums failed to take the hint. His comment, 'Why don't you come along if it's such a piece of bloody cake. In fact, you can have my seat, mate, and I'll have yours,' emanated from amongst the mass of airmen, by now almost out of sight in the haze of smoke. There was some safety in invisibility and an overseas accent. I imagined that Groundbound was probably developing a nervous tic by this stage.

'Can we have some order here, chaps, please?' This was from the squadron intelligence officer, a flight lieutenant who actually commanded significantly more respect than his relatively lowly rank and terrestrial duties would suggest. His appearance was, in some strange way, enhanced by an eye patch which masked the socket once occupied by his right eyeball. He had reluctantly parted company with it when a fragment of flak had penetrated his flying goggles over Berlin. He was truly ground-bound now, but in his case that was acceptable. The hubbub in the room faded.

There being no free seats on this maximum effort raid, Gordon and I stood at the side of the room, towards the front so that we could see what was going on. The great and the good of our squadron were sitting in a row on the raised platform at the front. Gordon did a double take looking at them. 'Bloody hell, that chap with the moustache next to the CO, that's Bobby Asquith, he was in my flight as a pilot officer, second pilot on Whitleys. He must be a flight commander now, he's got three rings. I'll be blowed.'

I didn't recognise the fellow so presumed he must have been new. Next to him was my old flight commander; he had been a decent enough cove and I was relieved to see he had thus far been spared the chop, though even so he must be reaching the end of his tour. I hope the dice continued to roll the right way for him.

The thought of staying for the whole of Groundbound's turgid delivery was more than I could stomach, so I went off to the watch office. I was interested to see to whom fell the honour of flying O-Orange tonight, so made my way to the ops board at the side of the large room. Running down the list, and noting the absence on this challenging op of the bold desk warrior Groundbound, I found the line for what I still thought of as 'my' Halifax. The pilot was one Sergeant Struthers, of whom I had never previously heard. At that time, many of our bombers were still piloted by NCOs, though before I left I'd heard that some squadrons were giving commissions to pilots straight away, apparently to recognise the responsibility of being captain of a four-engined, multi-crewed behemoth that was capable of destroying a medium sized factory on its own. I presumed that the old disdain in the Officers' Mess for anyone who wasn't born and bred an officer and a gentleman had, by now, been blasted out of existence. In any case, it was pretty certain that they wouldn't be able to enjoy their new-found status for very long, so they might as well be allowed to enjoy what little time they had. It seemed, in the case of our squadron, though, that Groundbound thought differently.

I returned to the briefing room and re-joined Gordon, who was following the proceedings with interest. The intelligence officer was pointing out in detail the numerous manifestations of nastiness that the Luftwaffe had put in place to confound us. 'My word, it's got a bit stickier than when I was here,' he muttered. In fact, he could have shouted it across the room for all the attention anyone would have paid, as long as we were still on our side of the invisible wall.

'You're telling me. It was Essen that did for us, remember? It's a malevolent pustule of a place, which should, in my humble opinion, be damned in perpetuity,' I offered. 'It is a source of considerable annoyance that I am still there and likely to remain in that festering hellhole for the foreseeable future, if not in perpetuity.'

The briefing ended and the crews went for their pre-ops meal, relieved of the obligation to listen attentively to a commanding officer they considered to be a wittering nincompoop. That was the opinion offered by yet another of the squadron's burgeoning population of Aussies.

Gordon and I kept to our plan and were at O-Orange's dispersal when the crew transport arrived to discharge the seven airmen whose fate would be inextricably linked to that of their aircraft. As the lorry drove off, leaving them with their kit on the concrete alongside O-Orange, I could tell at once that they were a sprog crew. We were mostly young, as I mentioned previously, but these lads looked it. We lurked nearby as Struthers, the skipper, tried to pull them together. 'This is it chaps. First op. I know we'd have preferred it to be somewhere other than Essen but there're no easy targets. We've been trained, we've been together as a crew for a while and we've got to get on with it.'

'Still in all, why bloody Essen?' replied one of his mates before wandering off to the edge of the pan where he was sick. Nerves, I thought. Don't worry old son, we've all been through it. I decided then and there to do my level best to help them come back.

I turned to Gordon. 'I'm going with them. It's all right for me, I know, but I want to keep an eye on them. They'll be bloody lambs to the slaughter otherwise.'

'Wish I could join you,' he replied. 'Unfortunately, I've never been in a Halifax so I can't get inside.'

The sprogs eventually climbed aboard their plane, and Gordon and I resumed our experiment in the deleterious effects of visible haunting on the outcome of an operational sortie, or however the boffins might describe it. Devoid of substance or not, we decided that it was best to stand out of reach of the four propellers that, once rotating, would happily decapitate anyone in their path. However, the start-up flare had not yet been fired and not much was going on, which might have been due to a delay. We were, therefore, still standing idly around when a staff car made its way along the perimeter track and stopped alongside us. The doors swung sharply open and from one side of the car emerged Bobby Asquith whilst the other side disgorged none other than Groundbound. He did not look best pleased to see us.

'What the deuce are you pair doing, hanging around like spare pricks at a wedding?', he demanded with his usual tact and decorum. 'Whose crew are you and why aren't you onboard your damned aircraft? The flare's due any minute now.'

I hadn't got a ready answer to that, as neither Gordon nor I had foreseen the eventuality of the squadron commander stopping for a chat. Not only that, but I didn't even know if I was capable of audible speech, as we'd never discussed that aspect of manifesting ourselves back in the physical realm. On impulse, I replied, 'We're spare bods, Sir. No one seemed to want us so we thought we'd come out here to wave this new crew off. Sprog crew, Sir, first op, but then I expect you know that.'

'Yes, um, well that's why I was here. To wish them all the best, and all that.' Groundbound was backtracking now. I wondered why Asquith wasn't flying on a maximum effort and hoped he wasn't learning the art of armchair leadership from the master. However, his loud sneeze suggested he had developed a head cold, which would have legitimately excused him.

After a further sneeze and a loud honk into his handkerchief, Asquith suddenly froze. He was staring at Gordon, as if seeing him for the first time.

'Good God!' he uttered eventually. 'Gordon Postlethwaite, isn't it? I thought you'd bought it when we were at my first outfit. When did you get back?'

Gordon coolly smiled back at Asquith. 'I came down in the drink and was fortunate enough to be scooped up by the fish heads. I got pneumonia so was laid up for quite a while and pitched up here last week.' As an actor, he was in a different league to Groundbound. He was also taking a chance that Groundbound didn't know the names of every crewman on his squadron. I reckoned that that was a fairly safe bet.

'Well, jolly good. Carry on, chaps. I'm sure we will be calling on your services very soon.' Asquith smiled and turned to join Groundbound who was his usual pompous self. With a harrumph, he turned on his heel and got back into the car, using the nearest door so that poor old Asquith had to walk back round. The Waaf driver gave us a quick grin, and drove off.

'That was interesting,' I ventured, once the staff car had left our immediate vicinity. 'Did you know we could speak to them?'

'I wasn't sure, but maybe it's because I knew Bobby Asquith. However it works, it seems to have done the trick.'

'What a good job we're in flying kit; at least we fit in,' I said. 'Speaking of which, I need to get in the Halifax, or they'll go without me. See you later.'

'Best of luck old son. You might not need it but they will. Look after them.' Gordon smiled and promptly disappeared.

I was starting to get the hang of switching between realms; I remembered climbing into my O-Orange at this dispersal, and simultaneously thought of the sprog crew inside their version of my old kite. Immediately I was there with them and it was still all too familiar. Every inch of the interior was the same as the previous O-Orange, though it was very strange to be sharing my workspace with an unknown crew. I hoped that I was invisible; it would have unnerved the lads to find they'd been joined by an eighth crewman, and even more so if they realised they were in the presence of a ghost. I'm not sure that would have done much to settle their nerves and I would have been even more at a loss for an explanation than I had been when ambushed by Groundbound. I decided it was best to keep a low profile.

Settled into their crew positions, the lads were kept busy with the endless procedures required to get their instrument of death and destruction safely into the air and en-route to the target. Out of habit, I lurked unseen alongside the wireless operator. He appeared reasonably competent as he checked the settings on the intricate array of gadgetry that the RAF had lent him for the evening. Once satisfied, he sat back and became lost in thought. That' I considered, was not good. He needed to keep busy and, above all, maintain his focus. If you stop and think at this point, there is too much to scramble your brains. You are committed now. You're inside a bomber laden with a few thousand pounds of high explosive and over a thousand gallons of petrol. That's not a healthy combination, even before you consider that there will be a bunch of highly-trained Nazis, armed to the teeth and hell-bent on killing you. Giving yourself time to contemplate the reality of your situation was definitely not conducive to retaining your sanity. I knew; I'd been there on several occasions. You have to kid yourself that you'll be OK, it's the other chaps in other planes that will get The Chop and it won't happen to you.

Fortunately for our wireless operator, the pilot must have spoken over the intercom because he snapped back to alertness and acknowledged, 'Wireless Operator here, Skipper. All set.' A moment or two later, the first of the Bristol Hercules engines coughed a few times and then caught, its sound rising to a steady roar. It was only one of four and it seemed louder than I had been used to. By the time all four motors had been fired up, I could hardly hear myself think.

Although I was apparently wearing my flying helmet with its traditional accoutrements; the built-in headphones, the oxygen mask and microphone, it was devoid of the insulation afforded by the real thing. I didn't know if that would change if I made myself visible but, as I mentioned, that really was not an option. I would have to put up with it. Knowing I could see and hear the world around me, I wondered if I would feel the cold once we got airborne. No doubt, I considered, I would find out in due course.

By now, the pilot must have seen the green flare as the Halifax roared even more and lurched forward briefly before throttling back and proceeding in a stately fashion along what I assumed was the perimeter track. Several minutes later we stopped, so I slipped past the navigator into the bomb aimer's compartment in the nose and had a look outside, as I had done on so many previous occasions. We were part of a lengthy line of bombers waiting to take our place at the end of the runway and launch ourselves into the sky. It was a strangely comforting feeling; so familiar in my old life even if it had given rise to so much apprehension last time round. I never realised at the time that I would actually miss it.

The take-off, when our turn came, was acceptable with a calm professionalism descending on the crew. I formed the impression that, despite their nerves, the crew had paid attention to their training and could operate the aircraft on a basic level. The next question was how they would react when under attack. I didn't think we would have long to wait for their baptism of fire.

I tried, as best as I could, to eavesdrop on the conversation between the crew on the intercom. The navigator and wireless operator seemed, from what I could see, to be speaking only when it was strictly necessary. Their discipline was good with no casual chatter and they appeared alert, though as this was their first op I would have been surprised if they lapsed into complacency before we had even reached the enemy coast. Over the din of the engines, I briefly heard the gunners, first the rear then the mid-upper, each fire a brief burst to test their Brownings. That was also something which brought back memories; I had been trained as an air gunner and, in fact, my post had been designated 'Wireless Operator / Air Gunner', usually abbreviated to WOP/AG. Once I even had the dubious honour of standing in on an op as rear gunner, when ours had a short spell in the sick bay. We found a spare WOP/AG so he and I tossed a coin to see who got the rear turret and who got the wireless. I lost and damned cold it was too. My hopes of having an easy time of it were dashed when we had been attacked by a nightfighter over Holland. He was a persistent so and so as well, making three or four attacks and I thought my last day had come, but fortunately he gave up the fight before I ran out of ammunition. It had been a close-run thing though, in the event, my last day had only been postponed for a month or so.

I reminisced for a while on the relatively fleeting period at the end of my life when this had been my own working environment. A couple of the lads had clerical jobs in civvie street before harking to the call of King and Country; they jocularly referred to the plane as our 'office', and that caught on. So much of a theme did it become that we bribed an artistic fitter, with a few beers to be consumed after the event, to paint the title 'Another Day at the Office' on the nose of the aircraft. Our attempts to get our callsign changed to O-Office was less successful and, after a rival crew derided our initiative by referring to the Hallie as O-Orifice, we gave it up as a bad job. To us, though, she was always The Office.

A small incident then sprang into my mind, taking on a sudden prominence. Our navigator had complained about various small items of his equipment seemingly doing their own thing when he wasn't looking. When he was busy with his sextant taking bearings from the stars, for example, his pencils might take it upon themselves to place themselves back in their bag. On other occasions, strange marks might appear on his chart, including on one occasion the annotation 'You are here', correctly placed at the aircraft's precise location. Once his chart folded itself up and tucked itself out of sight behind his parachute pack; on that occasion, he got rather stressed as knowing where we were really was the difference between life and death. I knew something was up as I was sitting at the wireless set near his own station and got the full benefit of his thoughts on the matter. When he eventually lifted the parachute, and found the neatly-folded chart his relief was palpable but his fury, initially aimed at me then all the other members of crew in turn, was intense. I swore blind that no one had been near his desk and suggested, with tact and diplomacy, that he was either going round the bend or that he should check his oxygen supply. It was a while before he saw the funny side and we talked about the occurrence for some time afterwards. No one else had witnessed the event and so the nav and I were accused by our mates of cooking up the whole thing. In the end, we put it down to gremlins, the peculiar paranormal beings that supposedly ran riot inside bombers, wreaking havoc with kit and equipment. Now was an ideal opportunity to test out a hypothesis that suddenly occurred to me. I waited until this plane's navigator had turned away from his desk for a moment then reached over, picked up the pencil he had been using to mark our position on his chart, and put it in his pencil case. I then zipped the case closed. It was a strange sensation as I couldn't lift either item in the conventional, physical, sense; it was more a matter of willing them to move. However, move they jolly well did. When the navigator turned back to his table, he looked for his pencil and it wasn't there. This he must have found baffling; I couldn't see his facial expression under his oxygen mask but he expended some considerable effort looking for it before opening his pencil case and locating the missing item. As soon as he turned away, I did the same thing again, just to make the point, with the same result, and then a third time just to make sure. This time, unable to immediately find it, he switched on his microphone and, looking at the wireless operator, mentioned something to him along the lines of 'Stop pissing around with my bloody pencil.' The wireless operator, with a shrug of his shoulders, suggested through his demeanour that he hadn't got the faintest idea what his colleague was going on about and that it might be beneficial to all concerned if he simply got on with marking his chart. I had little doubt that they would discuss this further if and when they returned to base. I was equally certain that, once they had been told about gremlins, they would agree on that as the cause.

I wondered who had been the ghost in our particular machine on that previous occasion, and why he had tried to interfere with the navigator's work. I could justify my experiment on the basis that I was testing a hypothesis; I wouldn't have dreamt of hiding his chart as that could have put the crew in serious danger, not to mention causing the benighted navigator to have a total meltdown. Then I thought of the other stories of gremlins and similarly unexplained happenings, many of which had caused malfunctions. Perhaps, I considered, the ghosts were simply trying keep the crews out of danger by rendering the aircraft mildly unserviceable so that it would have to return to base. Well meaning, perhaps, but the crew would still get a hard time from the bosses on their return. Even that was preferable to getting The Chop, you have to admit.

Bored now with winding up the navigator, I went to visit the gunners, not that they could see me. The mid-upper sat suspended under the glass dome of his hemispheric turret, seemingly alert as he swung to and fro in search of the enemy. Unfortunately, he was as much use as a chocolate teapot when it came to guarding against the real danger, an attack from the bomber's notorious blind spot below. However, it was helpful that he was still awake and ever-watchful for an attack from above the horizontal.

The loneliest post in a heavy bomber was the rear turret; remote by distance from the rest of the crew and entirely dependent on a functioning intercom to keep in touch with your mates. The rear gunner was often the first point of contact with an incoming enemy fighter and, as such, was particularly vulnerable. On the other hand, so long as you managed to grab your parachute pack, you had access to your own emergency exit, swinging the turret round and falling gracefully out of the back. Opinion was divided amongst members of this specific trade as to the best reaction to an incoming nightfighter. One popular school of thought was that, in the inky blackness of the night sky, the Hun pilot might not see you unless you opened fire, at which point the tracer would lead him directly to his target. Others believed fervently that giving the Jerry all you had, with four Browning machine guns, would convince him that you were alert and deadly, and that there were easier targets to attack. My own opinion was that it depended entirely on whether you were being attacked by an expert or a novice, as the latter would much more easily be frightened off than the former. But in either case you had a split second in which to decide based on your immediate assessment of how a fast-moving, small and deadly target was manoeuvring when you could barely make it out in the black expanse of night.

The rear turret is notoriously cramped but, fortunately, I now took up no physical space so was able to occupy it alongside the gunner who was, of course, blissfully unaware of my presence. He was scarcely visible as a human being under his bulky clothing, intended to protect him from the intense cold in the turret. As was common nowadays, there was a large area of the turret with no Perspex, the idea being that there was no surface on which ice could form or specks of dirt gather. The gunner was given a perfect view of the dark void, through which he hurtled backwards at over two hundred miles per hour. With the window open, so to speak, there was no protection from the outside air temperature which could be twenty or thirty degrees below freezing.

Within the void lurked the threat to the crew's survival. Hundreds of friendly bombers, focussed into a narrow stream a couple of miles wide and, perhaps, seventy miles long, surrounded our Halifax. If the crew was distracted, or injured, or visibility from the canopy was not good, it was all too easy for collisions to occur. Even more of a menace, though, were the night fighters. With a single engine, or more often two, they were faster and nimbler than we were. They also had the benefit of airborne interception radar so they could detect an individual aircraft from a mile or so away, close in until they could see us and then use their massively superior firepower to despatch us. The experienced fighter pilots would creep up until they were very close before opening fire, which gave them the element of surprise as well as a target that was almost impossible to miss. Their only concern then was that the ensuing explosion of an aircraft full of fuel and explosive would destroy them as well. For that reason, as well as the possibility of us firing back, their more novice colleagues would press the firing button from further away, their tracer giving us sufficient warning to shoot back.

My colleague was alert, constantly moving the guns and the turret as he had been taught. This would prevent the mechanisms from icing up as well as keeping him active. I couldn't see his eyes but I assumed they were constantly scanning the blackness for anything out of the ordinary. I did wonder, though, if he really knew what he was looking for. Once your eyes adjust to the darkness you find that, unless you are under or inside cloud, the starlight makes a slight but invaluable difference. The ground is featureless, as the whole of Europe these nights is blacked out, whilst the heavens are bedecked with jewels. Individually, the stars are pinpricks of light but collectively they will enable the alert gunner to differentiate between the almost solid nothingness of the earth and the slight reflection off the upper surface of an aircraft. It's far from obvious and all too easy to miss, but it is something. I hoped that his training, as a dedicated gunner rather than a part-timer like myself, would be sufficient to make the difference. It could save his life and those of his mates.

Looking upwards is more straightforward; once you are reasonably close in altitude to other aircraft, they will move across the starscape and you can get an idea where they are. Usually this works well for our opposite numbers in the *Luftwaffe*, handing them yet another advantage over us. Another factor is the position of the sun, ironically enough given that we are operating in the middle of the night. For some time after dusk and before dawn, the area of sky nearest the sun is discernibly less dark and it is quite possible to see aircraft silhouetted against the indigo. For our foes, once again, this can be very helpful and it is for that reason that the greatest peril lurks in the dark part of the sky.

Indeed, it was from there that our first brush with the enemy emerged. With frightening pace, an enemy night fighter flashed from starboard to port, a fleeting shadow that was gone as soon as it came. We had not been his target, mercifully, but some other poor devils were; off to port, which is the rear gunner's right, the flecks of tracer homed in towards the luckless bomber and crew that had come to his attention. The enemy's aim was either very good or extremely lucky. Almost immediately a flame emerged from an engine or the wing, tiny from our distance but it soon grew. We could not help them, just as they would not have been able to assist us. The flames spread along the wing as the volatile petrol played its enthusiastic part in the emerging conflagration. I hoped that some of the occupants, at least, had managed to escape from the stricken aircraft which arced downwards and then exploded in a red-orange ball, a cascade of green, white and red flares adding to the diabolical firework display. If the crew had not managed to get out unscathed, I now knew that somewhere an airfield was the unknowing host to another group of uniformed phantoms.

The enemy knew where we were, all right. Every couple of minutes, or so it seemed, another pyre would appear in the night and another bomber would make its flaming way to the ground. It occurred to me that the stars were holding steady in the view from the rear turret; this pilot had yet to learn that straight and steady was not the ideal way to fly in enemy-dominated skies. I wished, for his sake, that he would weave the aircraft, banking from side to side and constantly changing altitude and heading. It made life so much more difficult for the night fighter pilots, who might then go off to find someone easier to shoot down. Just now, I feared, that someone was us. This was what was so desperately selfish about the whole damned business; you just had to hope that someone else would get shot down instead.

I was at a loss to know what, if anything, I could do to help this crew survive their first op. I considered walking around the aircraft giving advice but I did realise that might cause some confusion. Gremlins was one thing but a helpful spook would probably take some explaining. I also pondered whether it was my place at all to try and save these lads from a premature end; perhaps there was a master plan and their demise was pre-ordained. In that case, who knows what chain of events might unfold if I interfered with their fate. I decided that I could but try; if their destiny was cast in tablets of stone, figuratively speaking, then I was probably far too small a player to change that. My problem, I realised, was that I had far too much time to think.

The next attack was sudden indeed; even I didn't see it coming. One moment the rear turret was an oasis of tranquillity, the next the gunner and I were showered in shards of Perspex as the panels shattered under a fusillade of German ammunition. It didn't affect me directly, I was too far beyond the pale for that, but I did find it just as terrifying as if I had still been mortal. The good news for me was that it didn't hurt and pieces of Perspex and metal from the frames and fittings simply passed through me. There was plenty of return fire from the mid-upper gunner but nothing from my mate down here. The Halifax was, by now, corkscrewing wildly so the pilot was very obviously in control and doing his best for us.

The gunner slumped back against the doors of the turret, blood visible as a shiny patch on his helmet, extending in a line surrounding a gash in the leather. It looked as if he had been hit with a glancing blow by a ricochet or a piece of shrapnel. Whatever the cause, he was out of it, for how long I didn't know. I just hoped it wasn't permanent, but as I hadn't been joined by his ethereal form in the turret, maybe he was still clinging on to life. I certainly hoped so.

I considered my immediate options. If I left him in situ, his mates would be unable to render any assistance to him, assuming they even got chance, that is. If I did nothing we would have lost a major part of our defence if the attacking fighter, or one of his mates, came back for another go. I needed to move him into the main fuselage and plug him into the oxygen system there; he might just hold his own.

Having moved the navigator's pencil earlier in the flight I knew that I could interact with physical objects. There was a massive difference in scale but it was worth a try. I grabbed the inert gunner under the armpits and moved back through the turret doors, dragging him with me. It took a major effort, though for me this was about concentration rather than physical endeavour. Eventually I got the gunner on to the bunk that was available for just such an occasion. Once he was in position I plugged his oxygen tube into the outlet and left him to it. I'd worry later about his reaction if he came round and went back to the turret, to where I now returned.

Now I had an intercom socket so connected my own lead to that. Fortuitously in the time since my reluctant departure no one at Handley Page Limited had seen fit to change the design and the thing worked. I could now hear the crew, very much on edge after the recent attack. They seemed to be aware of the rear gunner's silence, though not the reason why. The skipper was in conversation with the mid upper as I joined the merry throng.

'Did he not fire at all?'

'I don't think so skipper. I didn't see any muzzle flashes, but I was a tad busy myself. Do you want me to go back and check?'

'No thanks, mid-upper. That would leave us with no cover at all. I'll ask the flight engineer.'

I decided to offer some reassurance and hoped that they wouldn't notice any change in my voice. Fortunately the quality was magnificently poor and you could only make yourself heard by shouting. 'Rear gunner to skipper, I'm here all right. My turret took a pasting and dislodged my intercom lead. I've sorted it out for now.' No one commented that there was an interloper in the rear turret.

For a moment, I also thought about asking them to check the rear gunner who was, I assumed, still lying unconscious on the bunk, but I thought there would be little they could do that I hadn't already tried and they had their other duties to attend to. I felt strangely confident that, for now, he would be fine as and where he was.

I stared out into the void once more. I doubted that we would be left alone for long.

We weren't. Scanning from side to side, above and below, I made sure I searched for distant objects to maintain my long-distance focus. The danger of staring aimlessly into nothing is that eventually your eyes tend to focus at a nondescript point in space about ten feet outside the aircraft. If there was nothing else to see, I could swing the turret to one side or the other and look at the fins. I would prefer to be able to see another aircraft, ideally a friendly one. What I really needed to see was a smaller shape, as that would almost certainly be an enemy fighter. My best chance was to notice its movement across my field of view. Shape, shine, silhouette, shadow or movement; these are what our eyes have evolved to spot. In almost complete darkness, movement was the best bet.

I could, by now, make out a couple of bombers above and behind us and whilst focussing for a split second on the one that was almost directly astern of us, another sliver of black seemed to detach itself and move across to my right. Having picked it up I was just about able to track it as it grew in shape and its relative movement slowed then moved slowly back in towards me. It was growing because it was moving significantly faster and the rate of increase told me it was coming in fast. There was no point in waiting for it to show itself; I thumbed my mike switch and yelled 'FIGHTER!!!! SEVEN O'CLOCK, CORKSCREW PORT NOW!!!' My loud exhortation worked as the skipper didn't hesitate; the bomber lurched simultaneously to my right, given that I was facing backwards, and nose-dived. It then followed the prescribed rollercoaster course with admirable vigour. I was pleased once more that this particular pilot had learnt from his training and was clearly demonstrating an intense will to live. I hadn't fired, and neither did the mid-upper gunner, in the hope that the violent manoeuvres of the bomber would throw the enemy plane of our track. After a few corkscrews, I called up again, 'Rear gunner here, I can't see him, skipper.'

'Mid-upper, I can't see him either,' added my mate up on the top deck. The pilot eased out of our latest rolling dive and stabilised the aircraft.

'Thank you, gunners, keep your eyes peeled, chaps.' We had every intention of doing so, which was just as well as within seconds there he was, coming in like a steam train from above and to my left. 'FIGHTER, STARBOARD QUARTER HIGH, CORKSCREW STARBOARD!!!!!' I yelled this time, swinging the turret and its four Brownings round to my left, raising the sights and squeezing the trigger. The noise and the hammering was overwhelming as all four machine guns spat their .303 rounds in the direction of the fighter. As the Halifax fell away to starboard I caught a glimpse of the German fighter, which I recognised as a Junkers 88, flashing past at a strange angle as we were, once again, nose down. I saw the sparks of my rounds striking home on his fuselage. I doubted that they would have much of an effect; we had the aforementioned .303 bullets, almost guaranteed to bounce off whilst the Jerries had 20mm cannon which would rip us apart. As we came around to port and started climbing the mid-upper gunner shouted that he could see the Ju88 coming in again, this time from the aircraft's port quarter. Swinging my turret to that side I saw he was almost on top of us; this time the tracer from my guns went straight to the enemy aircraft and I couldn't miss. I saw the rounds hitting the nose and then his port engine which burst into flame. The Ju88 kept going without returning fire and I saw him diving away, eventually exploding. The crew saw it as well and allowed themselves a brief bout of cheering, until the skipper brought the festivities to a halt and suggested they get on with the business in hand.

There was going to be an interesting entry in the squadron's Operational Record Book, I thought, unless the rear gunner revived and could convince himself that he had just suffered a memory lapse. So far, the crew had been up to their eyes in hostile action and had no reason to believe that anyone other than their very own gunner was manning the rear turret. I wanted to go back and check up on the rightful occupant of the turret, I dared not leave the guns unmanned, for fear of another attack by the Luftwaffe's dark forces, this time likely to be lethal.

Fortunately, we were unmolested for the rest of the trip, so I was just an invisible passenger, journeying backwards over the blazing target and surrounding environs of the Third Reich. From what I could glean from the intercom, the crew carried out their first bombing run with almost textbook precision and I hoped fervently that their luck would hold for the rest of their tour. It was going to be a long twenty-nine trips for them, and they had had a taste of what was to come. My biggest worry on their behalf was that their rear gunner had, so far, missed out on the experience, though through no fault of his own.

Remembering my colleague, I went to his bunk as we took our place in the circuit awaiting clearance to land. He was very groggy but still breathing and he didn't seem to have lost too much blood. Dragging him out of the turret in the first place was a damned sight easier than getting him back in, facing in the right direction, but eventually I managed to get him on his feet. He was very unsteady, especially as the aircraft was moving around, but with my assistance he could wander in the direction of the turret. I opened the doors and propped him up against all the hardware. It was up to the mid-upper gunner now to provide any defence required but then again, without me, it would have fallen to him for the whole trip.

As we touched down with an almost satisfying firmness on the runway, I realised that I had now been on twenty-eight ops and would only have had to undertake a further two to complete my tour. That was, of course, a totally pointless consideration as I was still dead.

We taxied back to O-Orange's dispersal and I enjoyed the blessed and almost tangible silence that followed the four engines shutting down. The peace was then broken by the sounds of the crew relapsing into banter with the relief of having survived their first operation over enemy territory. Free of masks and intercoms, they could now talk or shout to each other, according to their positions in the plane. I gave the rear gunner a quick shake to try and get him to come round properly. Getting him out of the turret under his own steam was a bit of a tall order, and the invisible assistance I had rendered him earlier was no longer an option, if I was to avoid causing alarm and despondency to the other lads. They would have to come to him.

The mid-upper gunner was the first to notice anything amiss with his mate. I had, helpfully I hoped, left the turret doors ajar and as he alighted from his own perch and made his way to the crew hatch, he could see that the rear gunner was still in situ. He went back to his mate and asked if he was alright, being rewarded with a groan and a mumbled response for his trouble. The rear gunner was in more lively form than I had seen him at any time since he had copped the blow on the head, but that wasn't exactly saying much, as he had been comatose for virtually all that time.

The mid-upper shouted to the rest of the crew and I decided to leave them to it. I was confident that they would get it sorted. A quick trip to the sick bay and, with luck, no lasting damage. Most likely he would get a few days' rest to get over the concussion and allow the scalp wound to heal. If it was worse than it looked, a fractured skull perhaps, then he might get a longer break. If he was very lucky it might render him unfit for aircrew duties which, whilst undoubtedly disappointing to him in his naivety, would almost certainly save his life. At least he had the consolation of truly believing that he had shot down an enemy night fighter, once someone thought to tell him about it. I certainly wasn't going to disillusion him; dead men tell no tales.

Mentally and emotionally I left the Halifax and her by now blooded crew. Physically didn't come into it. Back on the concrete surface of the dispersal I saw Gordon, who had been biding his time getting up to goodness knows what, so went over to tell him all about the trip. He managed to look suitably impressed, especially when I regaled him with my account of shooting down the Ju88. 'Bloody good show, it was one of those blighters who did for me,' he told me. 'My rear gunner was a stickler for detail and usually managed to identify whatever it was that was trying to kill us at the time.'

'Do you ever see the other lads from your crew?' I asked Gordon.

'No, I've never caught up with any of them. We got hit by the Ju88 and caught fire almost immediately. He never came back round again, must have thought that it was a waste of ammo as we were going down in flames anyway. I told the lads to bale out and managed to hold the kite steady for long enough for them to get out, so I assume that they all made it to the ground in one piece. Naturally, I haven't got the foggiest what happened to them after that as the Lanc went into a spin and I was a goner. Maybe,' he added wistfully, 'we'll meet up again sometime but I sincerely hope for their sakes it's not for a while yet.'

I remembered I hadn't seen my own crew for what seemed an age but, in reality, was only the best part of a day. Somehow, I was sure they would have coped, but I did look forward to passing on my experiences to them.

Naturally enough, once I had, with Gordon's enthusiastic contributions, given the requisite lecture to my colleagues about what I had managed to do and how to set about it themselves, they could hardly contain themselves. It was a great wheeze. They took to the idea with alacrity and spread the word amongst the local spook community, which had grown considerably as we were joined by the ethereal members of other crews as they bought it. I can only imagine that RAF Elliston became the most over-manned airfield in England for a while, and it started to get a bit daft. Being invisible was fine, no one could see us and we weren't doing anyone any harm. Once we became visible, though, people in the old world could see us and it didn't take long for the Station Warrant Officer to lose his rag with all the spare bods who kept cropping up all over his previously-efficient airfield. We could swap between flying clobber and battledress depending on where we were haunting at the time and, when we were in blues, he could see our rank. To his intense chagrin there was nothing he could about the officers he started to encounter around almost every corner, except salute. This, inevitably, became a very popular pastime, as commissioned ghosts, on learning the whereabouts of the SWO, would lurk along his route in order to ensure that his right arm was kept bobbing up and down constantly. Our NCO fellow-travellers, conversely, did not have to salute him but had to endure a prolonged haranguing as he gave them a large piece of his bitter and twisted mind. They then learnt to gang up on him so that he would find himself surrounded by idling sergeants to berate. When he turned from one, who had just received some detailed advice and guidance, to sort out another, the first would promptly disappear to the bemusement of the SWO. After a few weeks of such japes, the SWO disappeared himself, presumably having applied for a posting to somewhere more sensible. I wished him luck finding such a place.

I had formed a sneaking suspicion that RAF Elliston was probably not alone in hosting so many former residents, all of whom were now at an eternal loose end. I recalled my previous posting to a Heavy Conversion Unit where we had learnt to operate the massive and ungainly Short Stirling, an aircraft we had learnt to love, particularly as we never took the operationally-challenged behemoth over enemy territory. Now at ease in the spirit world, I could recognise my kindred spirits and found that this old airfield was also home to many ghost airmen. There might not have been as many as at Elliston, as the latter was a bomber base whose airmen attracted the attentions of the Grim Reaper with monotonous regularity, but there were enough to prove the point. I then made a concerted effort to visit as many of the bases I had visited whilst on ops, to see if the situation was the same there. It was. Airfields the length of eastern England appeared to be full to the brim with disembodied aircrew, all of whom were at a loose end and potentially, therefore, getting up to no good. I assumed that many of the heavy bombers, by now conducting a massive onslaught against Germany, would also be conveying a host of unseen supernumerary crew. As we were weightless, we had no impact upon the performance of the aircraft, but reports of gremlins must have gone through the collective roof.

The weeks, months and, I presume, years passed though it did not weigh heavily on us. The clocks might as well have stood still, as indeed did our watches. We now noticed the passage of time only by the changes we could see through the misty veil that separated us from our former dimension. Buildings were constructed and others demolished, which led to a great deal of confusion as mortals could now walk through walls which were still as real to us as if they had been left intact. Meanwhile, we could move through those which were built after our death. We did get used to it; basically, if it looked substantial to us, it had been there when we were alive and was a boundary. Anything else was imaginary, as far as we were concerned.

The number of phantom aircrew peaked after a while, with several hundred of us milling around the place. Some of them were familiar faces from our time on ops, whilst others, like Gordon, were new acquaintances. Being dead was no barrier to socialising, it seemed, though the nature of our untimely demise meant that there were very few young women with us at this time. I would not have wished that they should join us too early; that would have been most unfair.

There came a time when operational activity back in the physical realm ceased overnight. I can only think that the war had ended. The absence of German uniforms and aircraft indicated that we had won, which did make the whole effort, including our sacrifice, seem worthwhile. I had gradually become entirely used to the idea of being dead, which was probably just as well as there was nothing I could do about it. If I felt sorry for anyone, I suppose, it was those poor souls who came over to our side very close to the end of hostilities. It would be bad enough to be the first person to be killed in a war, but the person to pity most is the last unlucky sod to lose his life.

With the end of ops came the departure of the Halifaxes. Whatever became of them was something I never found out but I should think the RAF had far more than it knew what to do with. In time, new aircraft arrived at Elliston, smaller and more streamlined in appearance. They didn't seem to have propellers either, so goodness knows what technology was now in place.

At least the lads and I could still conjure up our O-Orange whenever we fancied a trip out. By concentrating hard on a local flying route, we discovered that we could even make O-Orange visible to people on the ground. At first, we were ignored but as time went on, the reaction seemed somewhat more startled as if we were becoming less familiar to the onlookers. Perhaps they simply didn't see Halifaxes as often nowadays.

The ghost population, having peaked, now started to dwindle. I can't say why as we have no special insight. Maybe, with the war being over, more of our remains are being found as the wreckage of our crashed aircraft comes to light. All I know is that gradually fewer of us would be holding parties in the mess, lurking in the hangars or beating up the countryside in their old planes. I was talking to Gordon when his time came. In mid-conversation he told me, 'You know what, old boy, I get the distinct feeling that my time here is over. I have this tremendous sense of calm. Hopefully there's yet another side to this, and I'll see you there when it's your own time. Cheerio.'

At that, Gordon faded from view.

So, there you are; that is my story to date. It's been a good laugh, all in all, and I hope it is helpful to you. Perhaps you would care to visit Elliston, if you can still find it. Any other bomber station will do, there are quite a few of us still around. I hope you'll forgive the noise if we're having a party, and don't be alarmed if we walk through the odd new wall; it would just help if you left our surroundings as they are.

Also by Simon Hepworth

Shot dead on duty, PC Nick Kerridge wakes up in the Afterlife to find that he still has a job to do. The Grim Reaper is failing to meet his performance targets and recruits a team of cops to do the necessary work, tracking down people who are overstaying their welcome on the mortal coil.

Traveling back to his previous domain, Nick is curious to know how the investigation is progressing into his own murder. Not very well, is the answer, so he needs to help his former colleagues get back on track…

Available in paperback from Amazon and on Kindle.

About the Author

Simon Hepworth has had an abiding interest in the history of Bomber Command since learning, as a child, of the disappearance of his mother's uncle on operations. When the internet was invented it made research into such matters much easier, and he was able to investigate the loss of Sgt. Pete Gosnold and his crew. Once he had established what became of them, he set out to write the history of Sgt. Gosnold's unit, 514 Squadron. The result was two books. *Striking Through Clouds* took the squadron's Operational Record Book, transcribed by Andrew Porrelli and added details of every casualty suffered by the unit. He then wrote a narrative history of 514 Squadron, *Nothing Can Stop Us*, including personal memories and accounts contributed by Harry Dison who completed a tour of ops with the outfit in 1944. The book is the definitive account of the unit's war.

Simon Hepworth's first novel, *Late Shift*, is a satirical paranormal detective crime drama, representing a whole new genre which is intended to confuse librarians, who would not know which shelf to put it on, after one of their number told him to be quiet in his local library. Once again, the librarians had the last word; as fiction, the book was filed under H.

Married to the immensely long-suffering Mandy and with a son, William, Simon Hepworth has a day job, managing the deployment of helicopters and getting annoyed when they break down.

12577560R00136

Printed in Great Britain
by Amazon

The Dark Part of the Sky